TYRANTS OF
TIME

By
MILTON LESSER

I0616955

ARMCHAIR FICTION
PO Box 4369, Medford, Oregon 97504

*For more information about Armchair Books and products, visit our
website at...*

www.armchairfiction.com

*Or email us at...***armchairfiction@yahoo.com**

A WILD RACE AGAINST TIME WITH EARTH'S DESTINY AT THE FINISH LINE...

Do dictators rise to power by accident? What if their ascendency is planned throughout history by men of the future who play with time as if it were a toy? It was up to time agent Tedor Barwan to dig out the truth. But was the truth to be found in the present, the future, or the past? There was no way to no for sure until he locked horns with a female time fugitive wanted for criminal time-tinkering. Their jaunts into the past brought forth the horrible truth—that Earth's future lay squarely in the hands of a future tyrant, the likes of which rivaled even Stalin and Hitler.

Hold onto your seat as veteran sci-fi author Milton Lesser takes you on a wild roller coaster ride through time.

FOR A SECOND COMPLETE NOVEL, TURN TO PAGE 89

CAST OF CHARACTERS

TEDOR BARWAN
Can this time agent find the evidence that would solve the 20th Century crisis?

MULID RUSCAR
As Chief of the Time Agents, he was the aggressive enemy of all time tyrants—or was he?

DORLUP
He was being used as…what was the 20th century term he had picked up? …a fall guy.

LANIQ HADRIEN
Wanted for Time-Tinkering in several different centuries, her motives were a bit of a riddle.

VLADIMIR CHENKOV
Leader of the Communist Army, he climbed to glory over the slain bodies of his comrades.

GEORGI MALENKOV
One of the most powerful men on Earth. His enemies were everyone and everywhere.

STALIN
Yes, <u>that</u> Stalin. Transformed into a pink thing floating in a ghastly fluid in a little glass container…

CHAPTER ONE

SOMETHING buzzed in Tedor Barwan's right ear, driving the throbbing hum of the Eradrome momentarily away. In the sea of sound the rasp of the radio receiver buried in Tedor's mastoid bone was still unmistakable, and it alarmed him. He tongued the transmitter in his palate and said, "This is Barwan, go ahead."

There was nothing but the noise of the Eradrome, the shouts of the hawkers of a dozen centuries, the constant droning of the tourists garbed in costumes of fifty generations, the couriers noisily arranging guided family tours, the school teachers shepherding their squealing charges primly but still unable to hide their own eagerness. Tedor repeated, "Go ahead. Go ahead!" He'd dialed for a closed connection between himself and Fornswitthe previously; thus it was Fornswitthe who had tried to contact him.

Why?

"Tedor–help!" The voice hissed in his ear once then was silent. It was Fornswitthe, all right. Silent now.

Tedor took long strides toward the slidefloor. The Eradrome was so crowded that he couldn't break into a run. He was bone-weary from too much work and had come to the Eradrome for a few hours of relaxation, leaving Fornswitthe alone to start their report on the 20th century. The report was dynamite.

Tedor jostled his way along on the slidefloor; not content with its slow pace. The great green tinted bubble of the Eradrome soared five hundred feet into the air and burrowed twice that depth into the ground. Tedor was on one of the lower levels and knew it would take some time before he could reach the surface level.

"Busman's holiday, Barwan?"

Tedor whirled sharply before boarding the next ramp. He recognized the plump, thick-jowled face but could not tag it with a name.

"Something like that," Tedor admitted and kept walking.

"Never get enough of time traveling, eh?"

"Umm."

"In your blood, I suppose. Listen, Barwan. I'm doing a solidio-film on Time Agents. Would you mind if I hung around and—"

The name came to him then. Dorlup, a film writer. "I'm in a hurry," Tedor said, thinking of Fornswitthe's desperate call.

Dorlup puffed after him, "A little exercise will do me good. Haha. Not as slim as I used to be. What would you say to five thousand century notes for the exclusive rights to your next assignment?"

Tedor was interested in spite of himself. He was moving at top speed through the crowds and if Dorlup could keep up with him, they'd talk. "I thought the whole idea of solidio-films was to keep clear of time travel," Tedor said.

Dorlup puffed like a blowfish out of water, lighting a big cigar. "Used to be that way. But time's become the universal solvent. Business, pleasure, anything—all else is a dull routine. If the solidios don't turn to time, they'll go out of business in a couple of years."

"I'd like to help you, but the law requires secrecy. Besides, I'm in a hurry."

"I can keep up with you."

"Who told you I was here?"

"Coincidence."

"My foot."

"Well, Fornswitthe told me."

"What!"

"Fornswitthe, your assistant."

TEDOR paused on the slidefloor and Dorlup, his weight yielding considerable momentum, collided with him, Tedor grabbed the fat man's tunic and yanked him up on his toes, "All right, how did you find Fornswitthe?"

"I—I have my contacts. By Heaven, what's so important about that? You're hurting me, Tedor. You're causing a scene."

"I want to know."

"And I won't tell you."

"All right." Tedor let him go. "Get away from me. Go on, beat it."

A disgruntled Dorlup edged over toward the other side of the slidefloor, but Tedor called him back, "No, wait a minute. Who else knew where Fornswitthe could be found?"

"A lot of people. Secretaries. Directors. My producer. My comings and goings are no secret, Barwan. I merely told my associates I was going to visit Fornswitthe today and—"

"Today!"

"A little while ago."

"My comings and goings *are* secret," Tedor said bitterly, hurrying again along the slidefloor. "So are Fornswitthe's."

"I'll make a note of that," Dorlup promised.

"Haven't you done enough already? Someone on your staff talked. You talked. Either or both, Fornswitthe's in trouble, I hope you're satisfied, Dorlup."

"You're being melodramatic, I happen to know your territory is the 20th century; perhaps that's responsible for the way you talk. Couldn't be better for my purposes, you know. The Age of Atoms and Intrigue. Can't you see it now, in lights, glaring across a million solidio screens? *Atoms and Intrigue, The Life and Adventures of Tedor Barwan. Time Agent.* How about ten thousand? Wait, don't answer. What do you know about the year 1955?"

Tedor didn't even turn to look at him. He elbowed his way through the crowd.

"You know, man. You must know," Dorlup huffed and puffed but managed to hold a running conversation, mostly a monologue, "The mystery year, with a capital 'M' if I ever saw one. It's in your territory. If we can crack that particular barrier and do a solidio on 1955, we'd make a fortune. I'll split it with you. We could call it '1955!' Simple. Stark, to the point."

"Just what makes you think the 20th century is my territory?"

"Oh, experienced agents like you can't ever be tricked into talking, but younger men—"

Tedor clenched his fists, then calmed himself with an effort. "Because you had to visit Fornswitthe, he may be dead now."

"Really! It wasn't too hard to find his apartment, though why you Agents change your location every week is beyond me."

"Forget it," Tedor said. They had finally reached the last ramp, where pedestrian traffic was thinner. With Dorlup still shouting below him, Tedor began to sprint. He bowled over a middle-aged man but did not stop to apologize. Then he reached the surface of the green-tinted bubble and the starlight outside. He hailed a copter cab, gave the pilot Fornswitthe's current suburban address and was whisked aloft into the crowded local lanes.

HE found Fornswitthe dying on the floor of his study, a hole draining the life from his chest.

The lights were on, the windows opened, a brisk night breeze blowing the curtains into the room, Fornswitthe opened glassy eyes and tried to say something.

He was so young. So ridiculously young to be an Agent—even an Apprentice. A dying Agent, now, twenty-two years old.

Tedor propped a pillow under Fornswitthe's head, tried to staunch the flow of blood although he knew it was useless. Mechanically, he activated the transmitter buried in his palate, called Agent headquarters for help.

On the desk, a spool sat oddly askew in Fornswitthe's thinkwriter. Tedor switched it on, listened, "In 1955, Tedor believes the year a crucial one because..."

A fresh spool, barely started, and as useless to Tedor as it had been to Fornswitthe's assailants. There were no other spools.

Tedor heard a rustling behind him, close at hand. He started to turn when something plummeted down heavily and exploded against the side of his head. He staggered, began to fall. He knew he was fainting, struggling against the waves of vertigo long enough to turn completely around.

A woman stood there. She held what was left of a shattered vase in her hand, preparing to strike again. Tedor tried to reach her and managed a futile wave of his hand, which told her clearly a second blow was hardly necessary.

As Tedor fell, the woman's face etched itself into his memory. It spun into giddy unconsciousness with him and his last thought was that he would never forget it.

CHAPTER TWO

MULID RUSCAR wore a modern robe over his quaint 18th century sleeping gown. His sandals could have been ancient Greek. The cigarette he smoked probably originated in the 20th century, clearly the smokingest of all centuries. His sleepy scowl had a way of ignoring the centuries.

"Tedor, so it's you, I thought you'd started your report."

Ruscar, a tall, dignified man who fifteen years before might have been a solidio idol, snapped on the overhead lights. "You look tired, Tedor. I know when my men need a rest."

"Fornswitthe's dead," Tedor said, then told Ruscar what had happened. "So," he finished, "I came to, called the police and rushed straight here."

"Let me see your head."

"It's all right," said Tedor, revealing the blood-matted hair. "What do you know of a solidio writer name of Dorlup?"

"Friend of a friend. One of those things where you have to be nice. Don't tell me he had something to do with this?"

Tedor shrugged, "Coincidence maybe, I don't know. He admitted visiting Fornswitthe earlier. He's immensely interested in 1955."

"As you say, coincidence."

"That's hardly likely. Especially since Dorlup made it his business to know Fornswitthe's whereabouts. That's the part that hurts, Ruscar. If I hadn't decided to take the evening off, I'd have been helping Fornswitthe prepare the report."

"How far did he get?"

"Impossible to say. I found one spool, others probably were stolen."

Ruscar led Tedor to a chair, told him to sit down. Soon Ruscar had clamped an electrode to the side of Tedor's head, plugging the wire, which led from it into the wall. "Let's concentrate on this girl you found in Fornswitthe's place."

Tedor nodded, found it ridiculously easy. Moments later, a sheet of paper popped out of a slot in the wall. Ruscar retrieved it, stared at the sketch of a beautiful face. "She looks familiar," he said, and slid the drawing into a second slot.

He offered Tedor a cigarette, and together they waited. In five minutes, a buzzer purred, a section of a wall in front of them was bathed in light. On it appeared the twice life-size solidio of a woman.

"That's her!" Tedor cried, and read the legend under the picture. *Laniq Hadrien, age 25, height 5'6", weight 125, v. s. 36-24-36, hair blond, eyes blue. Wanted: 5th century B.C., 8th, 13th, 16th, 20th A.D. Time tinkering: pilfered fifteen valuable works of art, motive unknown.*

"I knew she looked familiar," said Ruscar after the picture had faded, "She's the daughter of a Domique Hadrien who created quite a furor a few years back with a theory about dictatorship. Maybe you remember it."

Tedor shook his head.

"Hadrien claimed one man or group of men in our time was behind all the great dictatorships throughout human history. Sort of—well, a monopoly on despotism. He maintained the position for years, getting cantankerous when no one in our office would believe him."

"What finally happened to him?"

"Disappeared. Last seen in the middle of your stamping ground, Tedor, but before your time. The 20th century."

"1955?" Tedor suggested.

"Possibly. Although I can't see a connection between that and Hadrien's pet theory."

"What about the theory, anyway?"

"WE checked into it, of course, that's our job, Tedor. We prevent time tinkering. A monopoly on despotism would be tinkering on the grand scale. For a couple of years it was a top priority job. We were never able to find out anything, so the old chief finally figured the whole thing was in Hadrien's imagination. A few years later I took over, and soon after that Hadrien disappeared.

"But you can bet we conducted a thorough investigation. You know what I think of tinkering, Tedor."

Tedor knew, Ruscar held his post as Chief of the Time Agents largely because of it.

"There is no crime worse than time tinkering. We are a people depending on time. Ours is a civilization, which exists in time. Many of our workers actually commute daily to past ages. Others live and work in the past entirely, paying their taxes and visiting here occasionally. We depend on the past for virtually all of our natural resources. Think for a moment, Tedor—"

It was Ruscar's favorite subject. Tedor had heard it before, but he found himself listening nevertheless, for Ruscar tackled this business of time tinkering with sincerity.

"Think for a moment what would happen if the past ages became aware of us. What would you do if you learned a group of men five thousand years unborn were stealing mineral wealth from under your nose, conducting tours through your backyard, exploiting you and your century for the far future?"

"I wouldn't like it."

"Exactly. So, the cardinal rule of time travel is this: don't get caught at it. When in, Rome do as the Romans do. Never let it be known you come from another time. And the second rule is an adjunct of the first: conduct yourself in such a manner as to alter the flow of time only sufficiently to obtain whatever is required from the particular century. Hence the crime of time tinkering.

"There's another reason for it, of course. Suppose history was changed. Suppose, for example, someone killed your great-great grandfather before he had the chance to sire your grandfather. What would happen?"

Tedor smiled, "You couldn't be talking to Agent G-20, I wouldn't exist."

"Precisely. You want this girl, this Laniq Hadrien, for personal reasons. She killed Fornswitthe, I want her for another reason. She is guilty of the one crime our culture cannot tolerate. She will be captured, Tedor. I'll assign a century agent to the job."

"No," said Tedor.

"Eh? What do you mean, no?"

"I want Laniq Hadrien. She's mine," If he lived forever he would never forget her face last night in Fornswitthe's place, with Fornswitthe dying on the floor, "I feel responsible, Ruscar. Forget the regulations this one time."

"Regulations clearly say the century agent is responsible for his own hundred years. Six to ten for a century, depending on its importance. Apprentices for each one, like you, all the agents did intensive work in their own hundred years, learning the culture, mores, traditions. You'd be at a terrible disadvantage if we let you go gallivanting all over time looking for the woman."

"I could always call on the century agents if I needed them," Tedor insisted. "They all have plenty of work as it is, and I'm due for a vacation. All right. Let me take the vacation my way. I want to look for Laniq Hadrien. If I can do the job alone, that would be a big help to the other agents."

"True."

"You have nothing to lose, Laniq was a fugitive before; she's a fugitive now. The fact that she's a murderer doesn't particularly interest you. Time tinkering is our line. But it interests me for personal reasons: I feel responsible for my Apprentice's death."

"That's reasonable."

Ruscar was weakening, Tedor could sense it. "You have nothing to lose, everything to gain. If I can find Laniq Hadrien while on vacation, no man-hours were lost. You're always talking about how few man-hours we have."

Ruscar laughed softly. "You win, Tedor. I won't send out a general alarm. I won't put any century agents on Laniq Hadrien—until your vacation ends. You have one month."

"I'll find her," Tedor promised.

"Don't be so grim about it. Quite possibly Laniq represents far more than herself. If her father disappeared in the mid-20th century, perhaps he does know something about 1955. Maybe Laniq does, too. I don't want you killing her."

"She's a murderer, not me. I'll get her for you, Ruscar."

Leaving Ruscar's apartment, Tedor rummaged through his pockets for a pack of cigarettes. Agenting in the 20th century had left him with the smoking habit—which made him think of Dorlup and his big cigars. What did Dorlup know about Laniq Hadrien?

Why was Dorlup so interested in 1955, the year time travel shunned like the plague. Not out of direct choice: after all its advance billing, 1955 would draw a horde of curiosity seekers if nothing else. But for some reason, no time traveler could penetrate the year. It was the one profound, inexplicable mystery of time-traveling, and coming at the peak of the 20th century cold war, it left a lot of questions unanswered. It presented two mysteries then. First, why couldn't time machinery operate there? Second, what had happened in that crucial year? Tedor wondered what Laniq Hadrien knew about it.

WHEN Tedor reached the far end of the pavilion, the crowds thinned to a trickle of people, most of whom were employed in the Eradrome. He entered a hallway and found a door marked with the words: *Executive Director, by appointment only.*

A pert receptionist looked up at him, "Yes, sir?"

"I'd like to see the Director."

"You have an appointment?"

"No."

"Then—"

"Here," Tedor reached into his pocket and withdrew his credentials.

The receptionist's face lit up, "You're an Agent! Did you know I've been working in the Eradrome five years and you're the first agent I've ever seen? I was beginning to think they didn't really exist. I'll tell the Director you're here, Mr. Barwan."

Moments later, Tedor was ushered into a plush office which borrowed its furnishings from half a dozen civilizations. Most of the furniture was what the 20th century called Swedish modern, but the carpeting was authentic 20th century. Persian, the drapes came from someplace in the Orient about five hundred years later, the pictures on the wall were replicas of drawings found in caves in southern France. The net result was garish but impressive.

Behind the birch desk sat a man of about forty, well groomed, graying at the temples.

"Good afternoon, Mr. Barwan. Cigar?"

"Twentieth century, I see."

"It's one of the most popular eras," the Director said.

"I'd like you to check on this woman for me," Tedor said hoping the Director would excuse his abrupt departure from the customary social banter, "It's urgent." Tedor gave the Director a picture of Laniq Hadrien and added, "We have reason to believe she's gone into time."

"Why, this is Laniq Hadrien! Certainly you know her father, Domique Hadrien…"

"Yes. His theory of a monopolist of despotism has given our department some wild goose chase headaches."

The Director nodded, pressed a buzzer on his desk. A young man entered the office a moment later, receiving the picture and a few terse words before departing. "It shouldn't take long," the Director told Tedor. "Did you also know that the Hadriens, father and daughter, are non-temps?"

"No, I didn't."

"Yes, non-temps."

The non-temps, Tedor knew, were a growing cult, which insisted time-travel was an evil both from the point of view of the ages visited, and of the age *doing* the visiting. They had gathered considerable data to prove their point, and although Tedor never looked into it thoroughly, some said they put up a convincing though completely impractical argument.

"We've got our hands full with Hadrien and his followers, just as you have," said the Director, "You can't argue with their figures, but sometimes figures don't tell, the entire story. Ten years ago, the non-temps will tell you, the population of Earth was one billion, far smaller than it was in the past because of a sensible policy of eugenics. Today the population is somewhat short of a billion, they say, and the census verifies it.

"Ten years ago, they continue, a quarter of a million people commuted into time daily to work in the various ages, sleeping here but working and vacationing else-when. Today the figure has grown to three-quarters of a *billion,* and it's still increasing.

"And seventy-five million people have vanished into the past. They simply preferred the past ages and broke all relations with the present. But that's the problem of you Agents, not us."

"Don't I know it!" Tedor said.

"The non-temps say this is a dangerous trend. They further maintain it is our own fault. We provide no real culture of our own, no sense of belonging. We gear everything to the past ages, converting our own world to a sort of administration center and nothing more. We work in

16

the past, receive our raw materials in the past; our art forms more and more are concerned with other times, other places. We do nothing to encourage living in our own century."

TEDOR frowned. "In a way, it's hard to argue with that."

"Precisely. They're leaving out one important fact, however: ours is a civilization, which exists not along the usual spatial lines but a civilization, which exists in time. That is a whole new concept, Tedor—something unique in the history of the world. If, for example, our ancestors had found life and conditions capable of supporting life on the planets of this solar system, we doubtless would have spread out to the planets and so geared our culture in that direction. No one would have complained. But the planets are sterile, and while we could mine them for minerals, the transportation cost is prohibitive. Instead, we have turned in an entirely new—and unexpected—direction.

"If you searched every inch of the Earth today from Baffin Island to the Antarctic continent, you would find no natural deposits of coal and oil. Silver is almost gone. Gold has vanished. The list is much larger, but you get the idea. With space travel fruitless, time alone can keep mankind going. If that is an evil, then so is the act of the first caveman who crawled from his cave to discover fire.

"Naturally, one doesn't steer civilization in a completely new direction and achieve perfection overnight. Perhaps we are attacking the problem incorrectly. The non-temps think so."

"Do you?" Tedor demanded.

The Director's eyes studied his, "That doesn't enter into it. We are interested in the non-temps because they would do away with the Eradrome and everything it stands for. This so-called monopolist of despotism is your problem. Ah, here we are."

The young man had returned with a small card in his hand. The Director read it and frowned, "I don't know how much good this information will be, Mr. Barwan. It seems Laniq Hadrien went into prehistoric times, exact destination uncertain."

"Alone?" Tedor asked.

"As far as we can tell, alone."

Tedor stood up, "Thanks a lot. At least I've got a lead."

"Good luck."

They shook hands and Tedor retraced his steps through the pavilion. He was already thinking in terms of the preparations for departure his trip would necessitate, but he couldn't get his mind off Fornswitthe's murder. Somewhere, some*when*, an unseen puppeteer held all the strings, playing them craftily but keeping the curtain of his little stage tightly closed. Little stage? Tedor shrugged, remembering Domique Hadrien's wild contention. Perhaps all of time waited beyond its dark footlights.

CHAPTER THREE

FAT Dorlup the solidio writer drank in local color like a starving cat laps up milk.

The time was 1954, the date Easter Sunday, the place, Fifth Avenue in New York, largest city in one of the two most powerful national states of the day.

Crowds jostled Dorlup. No one seemed to have anyplace to go, Dorlup least of all. The twentieth century suit he wore was tight and ill fitting; he was almost afraid a too-sudden move might burst his posterior from its tight confines. That's what you get for rushing, Dorlup thought irritably. But the Century Agent had frightened him. Damn those Agents with their high-handed ways, Dorlup was used to dealing with people, not martinets. He had extended the hand of friendship, even of financial gain, to Barwan, but it had been rejected coldly, unequivocally.

The Twentieth Century Corporation was another possibility, although Barwan would certainly offer a solidio audience more glamour. Well, when the city returned to normal tomorrow, Dorlup would offer the Corporation his proposition, though he realized sadly they would never be satisfied with the five thousand century notes he had offered the Agent.

"Hey, Dorlup! Oh you, Dorlup!"

The fat solidio writer whirled at the sound of the woman's voice, then groaned. Beti Sparr, a starlet who had been featured tragically (not in the story but in the gross profit, which was nil, Dorlup thought bitterly) pushed her way through the crowd toward him. Beti wore a costume of the day and wore it well. She had blond hair and looks and a figure. If, only she could act, thought Dorlup.

"Whatever are you doing here, Dorlup? My but you look silly in that suit." Beti entwined her arm in his.

"I'm doing research for a new solidio."

"Oh, but that's wonderful. I'm on vacation, you know, but I could learn the part while I'm here and—"

"My dear," said Dorlup icily, "I haven't considered casting yet. The solidio is just an idea in my head, and it will be a long time before I—"

"I can wait. Did you notice how positively garish the costumes are, how completely absorbed in their own importance the people seem?"

Beti had spoken in perfect hypno-sleep-induced English, and Dorlup said: "Quiet! Do you want them to hear you?"

"Oh, but they won't understand. They won't under*stand* anything. So—so archaic, I'm hungry, Dorlup."

"I'm not." He tried to move away, but the crowd pressed in all around, them and Beti still had her arm entwined in his.

"I've always wanted to try one of those automatic cafeterias. Shall we?"

Dorlup wanted passionately to say no, but Beti was already steering him toward the facade of one of the buildings.

"Sparr is rather remarkable," someone in the crowd said to someone else, "Whatever Dorlup is up to, she'll find out. But whoever would have suspected Dorlup is connected with the Century Agents, eh?"

"You can say that again. Leave it to Sparr, though."

Beti Sparr steered Dorlup into the automatic cafeteria, chattering and whispering in his ear.

Elsewhere in the state of New York, one of the forty-eight United States in the year 1954, a policeman on motorcycle chased a motorist, flagged him down and gave him a summons although in truth he had not violated the speed limit. This was his third such summons in a period of eighteen months, and under state law his driver's license would be revoked. He complained long and loud but to no avail. Actually, his life had been saved, for three months hence he was to be involved in a fatal automobile accident. The summons, which revoked his license, also revoked the need for his obituary.

He never knew this, but the policeman did. The policeman—not a policeman at all in the accepted twentieth century meaning of the word—was guilty of an act of time--tinkering. The man was an artist, though, a promising sculptor, and would in the next few years—if he lived—make a valuable contribution to twentieth century culture.

Thousands of miles away in a many-centuries-old tumble of gaunt, grim buildings called the Kremlin in a city named Moscow, capitol of Russia, the other great power in the twentieth century, a massive man with sallow, pallid face and a ponderous gait paced back and forth waiting for the state scientists to summon him. This was the half Tartar, Georgi

Malenkov, crushed by the weight of empire on his incapable shoulders. And when the scientists called, Malenkov plodded fearfully into a huge, windowless room where great, unfamiliar machinery throbbed strangely. What he encountered there was also a case of time-tinkering—but of an entirely different nature.

Malenkov stared in frightened fascination at the contents of a bell jar suspended from the ceiling and bathed in white, vaguely violet radiation.

A voice, metallic, far away, wavering, said: "Ahh, Georgi."

And Malenkov, heir to the mantle of Stalin and ruler of all the Russian people and their hundreds of millions of satellite subjects fell on his knees and cried, "It speaks! It speaks!"

Many hundreds of miles distant, in an unimportant place called Afghanistan, Domique Hadrien waited impatiently and with growing alarm for word from his daughter. He had chosen Afghanistan precisely for its unimportance. Although he knew Laniq was a capable girl; their adversaries were shrewd, merciless men possessed of a megalomania which would readily lead to acts of violence, Domique Hadrien decided to wait one day longer and then send his most experienced time traveler after Laniq.

CHAPTER FOUR

THE trail led to Ur of the Chaldees, to ancient Sumeria, to Babylonia, the cradle of civilization. Always Tedor arrived too late, always the angry little pip darting about on his chronoscreen indicated Laniq Hadrien was one step ahead of him.

But it was not until he left Second Dynasty Egypt that he noticed another pip on the screen. He was following Laniq, but so was someone else. Another saucer-shaped craft plied the time streams in their wake, making all the stops they made, starting up again when they did. Experimentally, Tedor thrust his own conveyor forward in time until he'd passed the girl and left her, decades behind him. The second conveyor became a frenzied pip on the screen, plummeting through the years with him.

The second conveyor did not follow Laniq Hadrien. It followed Tedor. He considered it and got nowhere. It failed to make sense. In the first place, privately owned time-craft were rare, belonging only to the few rich people who could afford them, to members of Laniq Hadrien's organization or to Time Agents. The century coaches carried most traffic through time, and no century coach would go off the well-traveled trails to follow Tedor.

One of the Hadrien woman's people? Perhaps, but he wouldn't have immediately accelerated through time to chase Tedor, not if he were trailing the woman for protection. A rich man on a pleasure jaunt? Hardly likely. Certainly not another Time Agent! Tedor scowled and turned his attention back to the girl. Laniq was landing.

Quickly, Tedor checked the time-charts, plugged in a hypnosleep spool, fastened the electrodes to his temples, drugged himself, and within an hour learned thoroughly the Attic Greek spoken by the denizens of the Fifth Century who had rubbed shoulders in the Agora with Socrates, Alcibiades and Pericles, five hundred years before Christ was born and some generations before Attica and its Athens were to feel the grim tread of the Macedonian phalanxes then of the Roman legions. Tedor ran the microfilm projector, found the pictures he sought, fed them into the slot of the matter duplicator and soon donned the mantle and tunic, the sandals and head band of an Athenian gentleman.

He stepped outside into a grove of Plane trees, found Laniq Hadrien's craft a hundred yards away but saw nothing of the third conveyor. Shrugging, he set out upon the road to

Athens, wondering how many minutes he was behind the girl. Other citizens walked the road with Tedor, some chatting aimlessly with him, others strolling by in polite silence because he had selected the garment of a high-ranking citizen and they were beneath his station.

The slave at the gate, an immense bronze man, skin and hair slick with olive oil, looked up from where he'd been resting his chin on the haft of his spear when Tedor asked, "Did you see an unescorted woman come through this gate?"

"Yes sir." The voice was deep, metallic of timbre, "A lone woman is unusual on these avenues, as you of course know." Women were second class citizens in Athens, remaining in their homes except on rare intervals and never venturing out alone unless they were so old and so ugly no men would care to look at them. "Further," the slave went on, "this girl carried a strange black box, which she pointed at me. I heard a clicking sound and wondered what kind of magic might dwell within it."

"You have nothing to fear," Tedor assured him. So Laniq Hadrien was taking pictures. "Which way did the woman go?"

"She asked the direction of the Agora. Again, most peculiar, as who does not know the location of the marketplace in Athens?"

TEDOR thanked him and set off at a fast pace down one of the main streets radiating from the gate. He reached the Agora merely by following the crowds and wended his way through the crowded marketplace with the shouts of the fish, bread, wine and honey-mongers on all sides of him.

The tradesmen jockeyed their pushcarts around for more advantageous positions; the slaves ran nimbly about the Agora on nameless errands; the gentlemen of leisure, garbed in embroidered tunics and mantles of white, red, purple and black, sauntered without hurry under the shade of the adjacent *stoas*, servants following behind them or preceding them like schools of pilot fish.

It was a hot day, the bright sun scorching everything and engendering an odor in the fish-carts which made the fish-mongers decidedly unpopular. Twice Tedor spotted Laniq ahead of him in tunic and mantle but with her hair free, snapping pictures with her camera, but each time the crowds swirled in ahead of him and he lost her.

The third time he shouted her name and she ran. He took off after her and tripped over something, stumbling against a fish-cart and overturning it. The vendor was an ugly old man with warts all over his face and a raspy voice. He threw a steady torrent of invective at Tedor, and in all these generations the meanings hadn't changed even if the sounds had. Tedor kept running, for he lacked Athenian money to pay the fish vendor. But by then he had lost Laniq Hadrien once more.

Her trail led him through all the stalls of the Agora but he did not see her again. He began to realize it would be foolish to remain in Athens any longer for fear he might lose her entirely when he became aware someone was following him. The man maintained two dozen paces distance between them. The man hurried when he hurried, slowed when he did, Tedor stopped, then turned swiftly and sprinted toward the mantled figure.

"All right," he said, gathering up a fistful of the mantle and holding the man. "Why were you following me?"

"I don't know what you're talking about. It's a free city."

"For citizens, it is," said Tedor harshly, "Whose son are you?" To say whose son you were was the equivalent of telling a man your name, since surnames were as yet unknown in Athens, Tedor suspected his follower, like Laniq and himself, did not belong in Athens.

He admired the man's poise. A vague suggestion of uneasiness crept over his eyes like a film, then he smiled and said, "I am Posicles, son of Posicles."

The slight pause was enough, however. "Get this straight," Tedor told him. "You'll deny any understanding of what I'm saying, but listen to me; I'm leaving Athens, I'm leaving Greece, I'm leaving this century, I don't want you following me. Is that clear?"

"Clearly, the Mysteries have befuddled your mind, my friend."

"If I see you again anyplace else I'm going to kill you. You live now only because I'm not altogether certain. Is *that* clear?"

"It is clear you are possessed."

Yes, the man had poise. Abruptly, Tedor struck him backhanded across the face and listened to him curse. It was an old trick, but like most old tricks, it worked. The man cursed fluently in Tedor's own language.

"Well, well, well," Tedor said. The man bolted and ran.

Tedor retraced his steps toward the gate, hoping he'd return to the grove of Plane trees ahead of Laniq Hadrien.

CHAPTER FIVE

BY the light of a crescent moon, Laniq found her conveyor, entered it, switched on a night light she knew would be swallowed by the darkness outside.

Stripping the mantle from her body, she walked to a cabinet and found her own clothing—shorts and blouse and sandals. Dropping her Grecian tunic to the floor she stood naked for a moment then climbed into her shorts.

Someone cleared his throat.

Laniq jumped as if she had been struck, plunged the room into darkness and remained absolutely silent. The room—the main cabin of the conveyor—measured twelve by twelve feet. There were cabinets, files, boxes, furniture. Ample place to hide. And someone—a man—was hiding there. A Grecian would have been frightened by the conveyor in all probability. Then had she been followed?

"Put on a light," a voice said.

Laniq gritted her teeth. She had no weapon, but even if she did, a wild shot might damage the conveyor's controls. "I'm not dressed," she told the darkness meaninglessly.

"Put the light on and get into the center of the room where I can see you. I'm carrying an atomic pistol and I won't hesitate to use it. I have another conveyor, you don't. If yours is damaged I won't care, I'm going to count to three."

Laniq found her blouse and began fumbling with the zipper.

"One."

Laniq got the blouse over her shoulder.

"Two."

Struggling to close the zipper now, Laniq groped for the light, found it, switched it on. She clambered into the center of the room, stumbling over something and falling flat. She sat up, groggy, unable to fasten the zipper and feeling every inch a helpless woman fighting against a cunning, ruthless foe in the time stream.

"That's better."

Laniq looked around, saw no one. She finally managed to fasten the zipper. She sat there, staring, "Well, where are you?"

Silence.

She was on the point of getting up and looking around despite the warning, when the conveyor door opened. She stared, mouth agape. A man entered the conveyor, nodded curtly at her and said, "Stay put." He waved an atomic pistol for emphasis, and since he had just come from outside and no anachronistic weapons were permitted outside conveyors, he was either a Century Agent or one of the monopolist's men.

Either way, Laniq was raging. He had fooled her with an obvious trick. Not wanting to be taken by surprise himself, he had merely planted an amplifier in her conveyor, waited till she entered, then addressed her from the safety of his own craft. He hadn't entered her conveyor until he was reasonably certain she would listen to him.

"Where are we going?" Laniq demanded as he set the controls, his back to her.

"Home to our own time," he said, and turned to face her.

WITH despair, she recognized the man she had struck in the dead Agent's apartment.

"Wait. Please," Laniq pleaded.

"What for? I've come over twenty-thousand years looking for you, I swore to find you ever since the night you killed my apprentice."

"Then you *are* an Agent."

"What did you think I was, Miss Hadrien?"

"Well, we were advised Fornswitthe and a man named Barwan had returned from the twentieth century with a report that would help our cause. Since there was a chance it would uncover this monopolist my farther has been talking about—uh, you know my father?"

"I know all about him."

"Anyway, we were watching Fornswitthe's place: It was left unguarded for not more than an hour, but that was enough, I returned in time to see you standing over Fornswitthe's body and...say! If you're not one of them, if you *are* an Agent, you must be Barwan."

Tedor nodded, continued adjusting the controls.

"Wait, Barwan. If you came twenty thousand years, then give me ten minutes."

"You didn't give Fornswitthe any kind of a chance," Tedor said bitterly.

"I thought *you* killed him!" she insisted. "But tell me, what did you find in the twentieth century?"

"That's none of your business."

"It is my business. If the Agents are going to sit by and let the biggest case of time-tinkering go on right in front of their noses, it's got to be someone's business, I take it you know my father's theory. All the most powerful dictators through history have not worked alone. Someone in our own time— we don't know who—has been helping them. If he could control the most powerful rulers in history, he could control the entire time-stream from the dawn of civilization to our own age. Labor, raw material, armies—all the world would be under his control. You found something in the twentieth century which substantiates that."

"Maybe," said Tedor.

"Maybe nothing. You found the Russians were getting outside aid—from our century."

"Even if I did—all right, I did—1955 is still the crucial year. I'm no different from anyone else. I can't enter 1955."

"Not in a time-conveyor, you can't. But you could set yourself down in the latter part of '54 and simply wait for '55 to roll around."

Tedor gasped audibly. "I never thought of that! No one did."

"My father did. He's there now. Listen to me, Barwan! There's so much going on that you Century Agents either know nothing about or do nothing about."

"What do you mean by that?"

"Clearly, this monopolist is a big-shot in our own day, with plenty of power."

"Dorlup?"

"I never heard of him."

"Solidio writer, but never mind. And this talk won't get you anywhere. You're going back with me."

"I didn't think it would. But I want to show you a few things," Laniq stood up, crossed the floor to him even though he waved the atomic pistol in warning. "Oh, put that thing away. If the fact that you're armed and I'm not stands between free world and slave world, you might as well go ahead and shoot me if it will make you happy."

LANIQ came so close Tedor could have reached out and touched her. The zipper on her blouse had been closed hastily halfway, revealing white throat and curving breasts.

"Give me the pistol," Laniq said.

Tedor looked at her, snorted in disbelief. But he put the weapon in his pocket and told her, "Go ahead and talk."

Laniq grasped his shoulder impulsively, "Barwan, you've got to listen! We can make a quick tour through time, just hitting the high spots, I can show you things; I can show you a man from our own time behind every important dictator in history. We've beaten them all along the line, so you don't have to worry about it. Except for the twentieth century. It's a crucial age, Barwan, and we're not winning. The whole course of future history might be changed if we don't."

"That's crazy. Future history already *is.*"

"I'm surprised at you. Why do you Agents make all that fuss about time-tinkering? There's no telling what might happen if history is changed—it's never gotten out of hand yet. But change its flow in the mid-twentieth century and we could be in for a mess of trouble. Maybe there's an alternate time-stream, perhaps we'll be thrust into it. I don't know—and neither do you."

29

What she said was perfectly true. Mulid Ruscar had always been very strong on that point. *Don't wait to find out,* he always said.

"Okay," Tedor told her, "All right, you win. We'll take this tour of yours. But remember this: I still think you know more about Fornswitthe's death than you're telling me. If you try to get away, I'll kill you. On the other hand, if you prove your point I have a month at my disposal. I can help you."

Laniq grinned happily, "I could kiss you, Barwan. Here, let me at those controls."

Tedor stepped aside and waited with mounting impatience while she set the time-conveyor for their first stop. Would Ruscar approve? He doubted it. Still, he was on vacation and he sensed a ring of sincerity in what Laniq had told him. He wondered how much her breathless beauty had to do with his decision, then found himself snorting again. He'd never lacked women, not as a Century Agent. But they'd always come to him, whining his name, begging almost. Laniq he would have to go and fetch.

And then Tedor felt the familiar sensation as the conveyor purred off into the time-stream.

CHAPTER SIX

"TURN of the century," said Laniq when they had stopped. "Eighth and ninth centuries A.D. Did you ever hear of Charlemagne?"

"Of course," Tedor nodded, "Ruler of the Franks, later of Germany, Italy; first emperor of the Holy Roman Empire."

"He needed help," Laniq said. "Come."

Tedor followed her outside into a murky summer night. The torch-lights of an ancient city pulsed and throbbed off to their left.

"His capital, Aix-la-Chapelle," said Laniq, "Charlemagne got help from the monopolist, Barwan. Fortunately, when Charles the Great died his Paladins couldn't hold the Empire together. Despite Papal acceptance, the Holy Roman Empire was a paper kingdom after Charlemagne."

Outside Tours proper, Charlemagne had set up a tent city in which the elite of his Army bivouacked. Clusters of tents dotted the plain, cook-fires cast eerie light, sentries prowled and plodded sleepily. Tedor heard loud talking in the old dialect of the Franks. Hypnosleep had yielded a new language to him again in a matter of minutes.

They crept up behind a sentry, were on the point of passing him when Laniq stumbled. The sentry whirled, spear poised, but Tedor ducked under it in the darkness and used the edge of his hand against the sentry's Adam's apple. It was dirty fighting, but necessary. The sentry went down silently and Tedor grabbed the spear before it could clatter.

"Stay here," he told Laniq. He had materialized for himself the clothing of a Frank warrior. With it and his spear he strode boldly to Charlemagne's own tent, relieving the sentry who paced outside it, then a few moments later relieving the guard inside.

"I don't know you," the man grumbled.

"I'm new," said Tedor. "German. Go to sleep."

Charlemagne was a tall, slender man fully six and a half feet in height, with white hair and a long white beard. He paced back and forth anxiously, great hands folded behind his richly robed back.

"The road to Rome is not open," he said to someone irritably, as if he had said it before but the man refused to take no for an answer.

"Not yet, it isn't," his guest answered suavely. He was a younger man, clean-shaven like Tedor, "I can open it for you. Empire awaits you, Charles; don't turn away from it."

"I still do not even know who you are."

"Nor will you—ever."

"What do you want if you help me attain this Empire?"

"Assistance. Troops if we demand them. Labor conscripted in your border countries. Certain minerals."

"Not gold?"

"Not gold."

Tedor stood his watch not a dozen feet from them at the entrance to the tent. The stranger might be from the future, although Tedor had seen nothing to prove it. He activated the transmitter embedded in his palate with his tongue and whispered almost inaudibly, "You are not alone."

Charlemagne had not heard him. The stranger could not have heard... either, unless he had a receiver in his ear. The stranger jumped as if stung, "Where are you?" Tedor heard in his ear, then watched as the stranger made a great show of clearing his throat.

"You are sure?" Charlemagne was saying, "No gold?"

Tedor never heard the answer. He fled back the way he had come, found Laniq crouching near one of the cook-fires.

"You might have escaped," he said.

"Did you see?"

"I saw, I knew you wouldn't try anything, I'm ready for another visit, Laniq."

Then was there indeed a monopolist? Ruscar had scoffed at the idea, Domique Hadrien had gone into hiding. The twentieth century, Laniq had said. But if Hadrien knew what he was talking about, Tedor must find more evidence and return with it to Ruscar. Once Ruscar had said something about tinkering on the grand scale. This made all other tinkering seem meaningless by comparison, and Tedor shuddered when he thought of the consequences it might have for the future. Laniq claimed they had beaten it in every age but Tedor's own stamping grounds, the twentieth century, but he knew that century alone could be more than sufficient, for it was one of the great turning points in history. Was that why Dorlup was interested?

"Come on," said Laniq.

"THE dialect you learned," she told him later, "is Yakka Mongol. This is the thirteenth century, Barwan. We are in the Gobi desert. You know of Genghis Kahn?"

"Of course. A Mongol leader who conquered all of Asia—his own Gobi, India, China. He moved on into Europe, too, sweeping the Russian, Polish and Hungarian Armies to defeat. He probably conquered more of the world than any other single man."

They stood on a high, windswept plateau with vast reaches of glistening white sand all around them. Legions of wind-driven dunes marched endlessly to the horizon, but a mile or so to the east reed-bordered ponds ruled over a verdantly green oasis. Surrounding the oasis was Genghis Kahn's city of yurts—the dwellings borrowing some of the features of the tent and some of the American aborigine tepees.

Dung-fires tainted the air with an unpleasant pungency. Strangely, Tedor discovered, there were no guards, no sentries.

"Their sentries have outposts on the desert," Laniq explained, "If a large body of horsemen arrives, they will see it in plenty of time. As for the lone traveler, he could he nothing but a friend. An enemy would not live long in this place."

They advanced on oasis, the unfamiliar yak-skin clothing itching Tedor's skin, the stain which converted him to a Mongol in appearance smarting in his eyes. Before long the black felt yurts were not ahead of them but all around them and they walked, completely uncontested, to the very door of Genghis Kahn's own yurt, the standard of the nine yak tails billowing above it in the stiff wind.

The Kha Khan, the Emperor of Mankind, the Power of God on Earth, the Master of Thrones and Crowns, the Mighty Manslayer—Genghis Kahn squatted, Oriental fashion, by his dung fire. With him were two men, the first old and bent, a scraggly white beard falling to his ornate belt. The second was younger and—Tedor may have imagined it—he seemed to be squirming and scratching in the yak-skin clothing.

"He can work magic," the ancient man declared, "I have seen him blast rocks. Oh Kahn, I have seen him make fire from a simple tube. Heed wisely his words. Oh Kahn."

Genghis Kahn wore long, plaited, greased red hair. His coarse, wind-beaten features worked themselves into a scowl. "He speaks fantasies," said the Kahn.

"Not fantasy," the third man at the fire said, sniffing distastefully, Tedor thought, at the dung-fumes. "Truth, I say this: Genghis Kahn can one day master all the world, from the Land of Morning Calm to the city called Vienna."

"Of Vienna I have never heard."

"One day you will," the younger man promised, "but sure, bold strokes are essential. The Shah of Persia would stop you. You balk at crossing his frontiers. You would return to Karakorum and rest."

"Yes. My capital is a beautiful city, and I *would* rest."

"You must never rest, not with all mankind ready to fall at your feet! The Shah of Persia anticipates border actions, clashes, sorties, patrols. Fool him. Strike with your entire army at the gateway city. It is far to the south of here, in a warmer land, but it is the gateway to the West for your people, Oh Kahn."

"Who is he?" Tedor whispered.

"Working for the monopolist, from our own time. Here in this age they call him Chepe Noyon and he is one of the Kahn's two greatest generals. Shh."

"I will lead your army, Oh Kahn. I, Chepe will lead it, and if I fall you may have me flayed."

"He can work magic," said the shaman.

"He had better," the Kahn declared dryly, "For we march from here to Karakorum to resupply our Army and from Karakorum we will take the southern route across the mountains to Tibet to the West. We will hit Bokhara in the spring."

The Kahn is wise," said Chepe Noyon, still scratching at his yak-skin garments.

"Let's get out of here," Tedor whispered.

But the shaman looked up, said; "And who are those two, that man and woman?"

Genghis Kahn shrugged imperial shoulders, Chepe shook his head.

"Then I say they are an evil omen."

"Ho!" roared Genghis Kahn, evidently more superstitious than history had suspected. "Detain them!"

YAKKA warriors converged on them. Tedor grabbed Laniq's hand and started running, fanning his atomic pistol's fire all around them. He caught a glimpse of Chepe Noyon's face, astonishment stamping the features, and then he forgot everything but the fact that they had to run—and hard—over the shifting, seething sand.

The desert was strewn with corpses, but the warriors kept coming, for life was cheap on the Gobi. Presently they showed sufficient imagination to keep well back out of range of the atomic pistol, however, and when Tedor and Laniq reached the time-conveyor they were alone.

They tumbled inside, Laniq running to the controls and Tedor bolting the door, Tedor would never forget Chepe Noyon's face as they departed. He did not have to say *you are not alone*. Clearly Chepe knew it.

"Enough!" Tedor cried, "I believe you," His head was whirling, but if the girl said her people had beaten the monopolist in all but the twentieth century, he wanted to go there at once.

She smiled at him, "No, I want to really convince you."

They watched Tamerlane's abortive attempt to repeat Genghis Kahn's Asiatic Conquest. They stood by while a man from the far future gave England's Cromwell the necessary encouragement for his *coup d'etat*. ("Cromwell's head will roll anyway," Laniq said cheerfully.) The pages of history came alive again when Napoleon cavorted for them at Elba, convinced by a man who appeared mysteriously out of nowhere to break the chains of his exile and try his hand once more at world empire. ("Thank God for Wellington.") They watched Kerensky's provisional government fall in the days of the Russian Revolution, paving the way for Communist dictatorship. But Kerensky was betrayed from within, and not by a Russian but a man from the future. ("We don't know about this one yet, Barwan.") And not the Germans in a secret railroad train, but men from the future in a time-conveyor, spirited Lenin back from Russia in time to assume the mantle of empire and so pave the way for Stalin and Malenkov.

"I want to show you one thing more before we head for the year 1954," Laniq told Tedor, whose head by now was swimming with a vast new—and sinister—concept of history. "Did you ever hear of Adolph Hitler?"

CHAPTER SEVEN

THE city was Munich in the early 1920's, narrow cobbled streets all a-clatter with horses and wagons and learning the new sound of the gasoline automobile and the swaying electric trolley. Munich, Germany, city of commerce, transportation hub noisy with the sounds of arrival and departure, its byways crowded with small homburgs, bicycles, checkered caps. The Munich of the Beer Halls and great steins of hearty German beer and singing and raucous laughter. But also the Munich of unrest, distrust, intense intellectual turmoil, and the Munich which, not many months later, was to be the scene of the abortive *putsch* in a beer cellar which started a slight little man with stray-locked dark hair on his path toward world conquest.

They sat in a beer hall, Laniq and Tedor, and at a table near them sat a man, young but with eyes which to Tedor were at once the most fiery, most intense and oldest he had even seen. He was a man, Tedor guessed, who would never know a tranquil moment in his life; cold, friendless, fidgety, smoldering with nameless resentments.

"That's Hitler," Laniq said unnecessarily, "It is why we have come here."

They had spent three hours in the beer cellar so often frequented by Hitler, a second-rate poster artist, ex-Army corporal and smoldering revolutionary.

A man came to the table and joined Hitler, not half a dozen feet from where Laniq and Tedor sat with their beer. As the one was stamped with his personality as clearly as ever a man could be, so the other was poker-faced nondescript, neither German nor non-German, feverish agitator nor tranquil pacifist.

"You have come," said Hitler, easily loud enough for Tedor to hear. "It is good, I have spent the entire day thinking of what you have told me. It is like a storm bursting inside of me, a happy torment, as if it holds the seeds of a strife which can make everything clear, lucidly clear for Germany and the world, their destiny, one the master the other the follower. You will one day be a great man."

"Not I, Adolph. You harbor the inherent qualities for greatness."

"I know," said Hitler, and made it sound the most natural thing in the world, "I was born for greatness, I will be great. But you have earned it with your perception, your understanding, with your ability to point out objectively what I could not see for my raging emotions."

"It is only common sense, Adolph. You had the idea; clearly, the idea was in you. A year, two years, it would have materialized. I merely acted like a catalyst."

"To the East," said Hitler in a dreamy voice, all the while his eyes burned furiously, "is the Bolshevik, the Red Scourge, the hated, feared enemy of mankind. To the West is the Democratic world, the England of many centuries, the France of polite ways and laughable indecisions, the young America, still trying its wings.

"Which is the enemy of the people? I will tell you which. It is as you have said. The Red, the Communist Bolshevik is the enemy of the people. Tell them, 'See, the Red is coming!' and they will run, to arms, defending their homes and what they love as if it were Ragnarok itself. Good. We will tell them that.

"And which is the enemy of Hitler, the real enemy of Hitler who—as you say—was born to lead Germany, the Third Reich, to world glory? It is not the Red Bolshevik, no. It is the West, with its standard of living, its broad, idealistic aims which while incapable of bearing fruit are nevertheless infinitely attractive; the West with its showcase democracy, the West with its guaranteed personal liberties for morons and sub-morons, the West which yearns after the individual to the neglect of the state and so makes all individuals everywhere yearn so too.

"I will fire my people with hatred for the Red when hatred for the Jew has weakened because one day we will exterminate the Jew. The one is a legitimate hatred, the other a fancied one—but with the fires once stoked, the hatred will burn brightly. When it turns, as assuredly it will, to still a third and now unthinkable hatred, frenzy will ride high the crest of a wave—and the legions of the Third Reich will turn suddenly and devastatingly on the West, which today the German people cannot hate but which will one day bear the brunt of their hatred and power and rage because I, Hitler, tell them so."

"I am glad I could bring this to the surface in you so much sooner than it otherwise might have appeared," said the nondescript man.

"You are glad? *You?"* Tears streamed down Hitler's face, yet he laughed. "Think how I feel. I, Hitler. A man today, a God tomorrow, because you showed me the way. Name your price, request your reward; when the world is mine the half you want shall be yours."

"I want only what is best for Germany and its people," said the man.

"What he means," Laniq whispered to Tedor, "is he wants what is best for the monopolist. Naturally he's one of our own people. Fortunately for the world, he drove this point home too strongly. Hitler will move, and soon, making a wild, incredible bid for power. When it aborts, he will bide his time for another decade, giving the free world additional time to prepare."

"Why don't we wait for him outside, take him, and see what we can learn?" Tedor demanded.

"Risk everything on that when we know Hitler will fail? This man probably doesn't know the monopolist, anyway. He is a shadow figure, a ghost. None of them knows his identity, at least that has been my experience."

"Still—"

"Still nothing. The twentieth century's middle years are the significant ones. Let all else ride if we must, for it is there the monopolist will either succeed or fail with plans that will make the dreams of a dozen Hitlers seem something less than child's play."

"Okay, Laniq. You win. But remember this; once we get to my stamping grounds, I'm going to take over. Brief me if you want to, but I have the contacts. Besides, I came hell-bent into the time-stream looking for you and now I find apparently all my ideas need readjusting. I'll be able to think a lot better with some affirmative action under my belt."

"Very well. What do we do first?"

"Well, now—"

"We seek out my father in Afghanistan, naturally. He can do the briefing you suggest. After that…"

"After that I take over," Tedor growled, then smiled, "Come on."

CHAPTER EIGHT

"MY father's followers needed an out-of-the-way place like this," Laniq explained as the time-conveyor dropped out of the time-stream and cruised along above the desert. "We're building a spaceship, you see."

"A spaceship? What for? There is nothing worth while on the planets, nothing worth the trouble to mine it."

"My fault, Tedor, I should have said a starship. If necessary, we'll go to the stars. Oh, we can do it, although the trip will take generations and only a few hundred people will find room. We won't do it unless the monopolist forces us. If he gains the dictatorial control of time he's seeking, we'll have no choice. We're collecting trophies, artifacts of man's culture, just in case. We'll gladly put them in a museum or return them if the monopolist fails." Laniq turned to the port, gazed down on the desert sweeping by. Suddenly; "Tedor!"

Tedor stood beside her and stared down. There had been a village of tents below them. There now were the remains of tents in a well-watered oasis—but no village.

Fires smoldered below them. Charred wreckage lay strewn about the rolling dunes and jumbled rock on either side of the oasis. A great silver hull—the body of an incomplete starship, Tedor knew, lay on its side, a dying animal, huge rents and gashes disfiguring it like ugly, bloodless scars.

"Tedor—Tedor—I'm afraid!"

Tedor took the conveyor down, landing it adjacent to the wrecked starship. He climbed out first, helped Laniq alight. Dazed, clasping and unclasping her hands, she walked about the oasis. In some of the burned tents dishes were set on crude tables. Personal equipment was everywhere, on the floors, on the charred plastoid beds, in hastily emptied lockers. Most of the fires had burned themselves out, but smoke still curled lazily into the dry, hot air of the desert.

"They came, Tedor. They destroyed—everything."

Tedor stood mutely, uncomfortably, not knowing what to say. Everything he thought about Laniq had changed so drastically in the space of a few hours and now he wanted to help her, but could do nothing.

"Miss Hadrien. Miss Hadrien!"

They whirled together, saw a dark head poke itself out from behind one end of the spaceship, large burnoose very white over the brown skin. It was a boy of perhaps fourteen.

He was trembling, his lips puckered. He sobbed. "Oh, Miss Hadrien…"

Laniq went to him, patted his shoulder. "Mahmud, there now, it must have been awful, I know. There, Mahmud."

With someone to comfort him, Mahmud cried all the more. He railed loudly, letting the tears gush down his cheeks, abandoning his body to wracking sobs.

Tedor who spoke Persian and understood it, realized the boy would go right on crying and Laniq comforting him and so not finding time to cry herself. And so he aid, "Mahmud, tell me what happened. Tell me where Miss Hadrien's people are."

Mahmud sniffled, blinked his eyes, plucked a handful of gummy dates from the folds of his burnoose. He munched, sniffled again. "Dead," he sobbed. "They are all dead, almost."

Laniq sobbed too, clutching little Mahmud's shoulder more firmly. "Dead?" she cried. "Dead? Where?"

"Maybe not all, Miss Hadrien. Those that could, fled— taking the dead with them. It happened not long ago when three round craft came down from the sky and burned everything. They struck without warning. My people fled."

"You are very brave, Mahmud," Laniq declared, "What— happened to my father?"

"The Hadrien Sir was badly hurt, Miss. Of that much I am sure. They carried him with much moaning and bleeding into their craft, your people did, and went to the West. 'Laniq' he kept mumbling. He looked at me while they carried him and said 'Laniq! You tell Laniq we went to Nevada. She'll know where. Tell Laniq we went to Nevada, but tell no one else.' That is what he said and I Mahmud, remember every word."

"Thank, you, Mahmud. And what about you?"

Mahmud smiled for the first time. "Oh, presently I will return among my people who fled in the face of all this terror from the sky. But it will not be the same."

"It will be the same," said Laniq. "They are your people."

"I say it will not be the same, but thank you, Miss. I will go among my people with my great sadness and remember yours forever."

"If I thought you would be happy, I would take you with me."

"Miss—"Mahmud looked at her hopefully.

"No, Mahmud. You won't understand this, not yet. But they are your people, your home and your world. You could not pick up the threads of a new life and a new way of life without sorrow. Your people did what anyone else would have done, including *my* people. They had their own homes to protect; they could not throw their lives away vainly in my people's defense."

Mahmud smiled again, then turned to go. "I was hoping you would say that, Miss Hadrien." He trotted off with head high and shoulders squared.

"He'll be all right, I think," Laniq said. "We'd better get to Nevada, Tedor."

Together they ran for the time-conveyor. It hurt her not to, but Laniq never looked back at the devastated community.

CHAPTER NINE

"SEVENTEEN, red," fat Dorlup proclaimed to the croupier in a Reno gambling joint.

The wheel spun, the ball clicked, rattled, jumped with it.

"Seventeen, red," declared the croupier in an awed voice as he raked a tall stack of chips toward the one Dorlup had placed in the red seventeen. Dorlup gathered the stack in with his pudgy arms and deposited it carelessly in the growing mountain of chips nearby.

"You're wonderful," the honey-blond solidio actress told him, squeezing his arm to add emphasis.

There was no shaking Beti, not since that day, months ago, when she had steered Dorlup into the Automat in New York. Since then he had been across the country three times, and she with him. He had gained a lot of source material for his solidio, and it amused him after a few days when he realized Beti was spying on him for someone. He didn't care, since he had nothing in particular to hide. And, anyway, there were certain joys of which Beti was truly the mistress, despite the vacuum, which seemed to exist inside her skull.

"You *are* wonderful," Beti said again.

Dorlup patted her hand without real affection. "Everyone in here thinks I have a system. *The* system to beat the game, I might add. There is only one system. I know that system. Roulette wouldn't have a chance where we come from."

"It all rides on eight, black," Dorlup told the croupier.

"All?" The man's polish had cracked.

"All."

"Eight black," the croupier intoned a moment later. The crowd ooh'ed and aah'ed.

"Well," said Dorlup, and gathered in the chips again.

"Mr. Dorlup?" someone at his shoulder asked.

"Yes, I am Dorlup. What do you want?"

"Come with me."

"What for?"

"Don't make a scene, Mr. Dorlup," the man said in a soft voice. Then in a language, which Dorlup had not heard for six months: "It is important that I talk with you."

Dorlup's eyes bulged, "You're an Agent?"

"Come with me, please."

Dorlup told Beti to play with his chips, then followed the man from the gambling room into the bar.

"Scotch," said Dorlup with a smile. "Might as well be your treat, eh?"

"Two scotches, then," said the man. "You're in serious trouble, Dorlup."

"Is that so?"

"Quite. For a long time the Century Agents have played down stories about a time-tinkerer who had broken more rules than all the tinkerers before him. He was called the monopolist of despotism, although frankly the Agents neither invented nor particularly cared for the term. We played down the stories but we hardly doubted them. As I said, you are in trouble, Dorlup. You are under arrest."

"This is fantastic. What's the charge?"

"Time tinkering, of course. You are the monopolist, Dorlup."

"What? WHAT?"

"You are the monopolist."

Beti played with Dorlup's chips until not one remained in front of her. The croupier was his old self again, calm, detached, indifferent. She looked all around the club for Dorlup but couldn't find him.

No doubt the stranger had been an Agent. Beti hardly understood all that had happened in the last few months. First they told her to spy on Dorlup and she had—gladly, since she had done other small jobs for them in the past and the pay was good. *I'm not as dumb as he thinks*, she thought with a smile. And then, then they had told her to lie in her reports. She had lied cheerfully, at their direction. But why did they need to spy if she spied and found nothing, then reported all sorts of things? She shrugged her shapely shoulders. They had their reasons.

They also had Dorlup, she concluded. Then her job was finished.

She had a drink, listened to a sultry-voiced girl render the latest popular song, and went outside into the cool night air. A sleek car roared to a quick stop in front of her. The back door opened. "Get in," someone said in the darkness.

She hesitated. Hands reached out, tugged at her, pulled her. She was too surprised to try fighting them off, but they were big, strong hands and it would have been futile anyway. She was deposited on the back seat of the car, between two men. The one on her right she had never seen before. She had seen pictures of the one on her left, the handsome man who was approaching middle age so attractively.

He was Mulid Ruscar, Chief of the Century Agents.

CHAPTER TEN

"WHERE'S my father?" Laniq demanded.

"I'll take you to him." The man led them down a street lined with prefabricated, Quonset-like houses. People smiled at Laniq, but wanly and most of the houses were deserted.

An old man shook his head sadly, said, "There was great carnage in Afghanistan. We don't know how it happened, we can only guess. Someone was followed, despite all our efforts."

They walked on, came at last to one of the prefabricated dwellings which seemed no different from all the others. It was late autumn, 1954, but here in southern Nevada, warm winds swept uncomfortably through the dusty street.

A short, stocky man met them at the door. "You'll have to be quiet," he said.

"Dr. Jangor, how is my father?"

"Badly hurt, I'm afraid. He'll live, but we had to amputate his right leg above the knee. Come in, child."

Tedor followed Laniq awkwardly inside.

"He's in there," the doctor said, pointing to a closed door.

"I'd better wait outside," Tedor told Laniq.

"No, I want you with me."

Shrugging, Tedor followed her within the room. His head propped on pillows, a man lay in the single bed. He was neither awake, nor asleep, but in that halfway state, semi-conscious, dreamy, yet extremely lucid.

"He's been doped against the pain," said Dr. Jangor, and closed the door behind him.

"Dad," Laniq called softly.

The head on the pillow stirred. Sweat beaded the skin, ran into the eyes and made them squint.

"Dad, it's Laniq."

The lips hardly moved, but Tedor heard: "La-niq? Laniq, you've come back."

She knelt by the bed, let her hand rest on her father's feverish brow. "It's all right now, Dad. Everything's going to be all right."

"They destroyed the starship, Laniq. Completely. We—don't have that way out any longer. We've got to beat the monopolist in Russia. It's his last chance." Domique Hadrien spoke without heat, with no emotion at all. The words spilled from his lips one after the other, tonelessly. "We have beaten him all along the line, without even knowing his identity. But he has the best chance in Russia and knows it.

"We approach 1955, the crucial year. I said it was the monopolist's last chance. Well, it is ours as well. If he wins in Russia, if he goes on to unite the whole 20th century world as a Russian slave state, then he's on his way toward ultimate conquest of all time. Think of the power at his disposal: an Army to be drawn from two and a half billion people. We must stop him.

"Who is with you, Laniq?"

"A friend," Laniq assured him. "You can talk."

"I—I know what we have to do. A one-legged man, recuperating, isn't good for much. Someone must go to Russia and—"

"I can go," Tedor said. "I have contacts there. Century Agents."

"I'll go with you," Laniq told him.

"You'll stay right here."

"Yes? What would you do in Russia?"

"Well—"

"Do you have a plan?"

"Of course not yet. But I could see what's happening—"

DOMIQUE Hadrien seemed more clearly awake, more alert. "Nonsense, young man. When it comes to intrigue, Laniq is as capable as a man. Further, she knows what we've been planning all along."

"What's that?"

"If you're familiar with their recent history, you'll recall that their former dictator, Stalin, died early last year. The new premier, Malenkov, is a man to his people, where Stalin was a god. With their effective propaganda-indoctrination machines, I don't doubt Malenkov will one day also be regarded almost as a deity—if we give them time. That's what the monopolist wants, naturally. It's a necessary part of his plans. But Chenkov, the new Army Chief is backed by a strong military clique, which would like him and not Malenkov to assume the mantle of godhood. As for the people, they were willing to take what Stalin dished out because Stalin was their god; but Malenkov is not only a man but a hated half-Tartar, and the people grumble whenever they have to tighten their belts another notch.

"So, Malenkov will one day have godhood. That was their original plan, but there is another development paralleling it. Wild claims have come out of Russia, rumors, whispered talk—all saying that Stalin, miraculously, is living again. It's sheer imagination, I suspect. It's an attempt to pan a make believe Stalin off on the people in case Malenkov falls on his face while playing God."

"Then we go to Moscow," said Tedor, "as Russians, of course. We must discredit Malenkov where possible, disprove the Stalin-rebirth theory—"

"And incite the people to revolt," Laniq finished for him.

"Well," said Tedor, and smiled.

"It isn't as difficult as it looks, although I think I'd rather go hunting for lions with my bare hands. You see, I've been to Russia before, several times, and for the same reason. I have a fictitious identity there, which I assume on arrival. I've managed to snag a few top men as—uh, admirers. That includes Vladimir Chenkov, by the way."

"Sounds better already. You stay with your father," said Tedor, "for a while. I'm taking a trip up to New York to get some information from our Century Agent there. Then I'll return, pick up one female intriguer out here in Nevada, and we'll be on our way. Take care of yourselves." And Tedor left.

"Nice chap," Hadrien told his daughter.

She smiled at him. "You know something Dad? I'm just beginning to realize that. Very nice."

CHAPTER ELEVEN

THE office was on the twenty-third floor of a big office building in mid-town New York, room 2307. It came with all the standard equipment, desks, filing cabinets, chairs, phones, and an attractive secretary.

"I'd like to see Mr. Sertant," Tedor told the secretary, who was leafing through one magazine with half a dozen others waiting their turn.

"Isn't a very busy office," she told him flushing slightly.

"I didn't think it would be."

"You know Mr. Sertant?"

"We're old friends," Tedor assured her. It wasn't the truth, for he'd never met Sertant, although he had heard of the Agent.

"Then can you do me a favor, Mister?"

"Maybe."

"What does he do? I mean, what's Mr. Sertant's business? The way he snoops around people sometimes, you'd think he was a private detective. You know, like Mike Hammer?"

"You might call him that."

"I just wanted to know if I could tell my friends I'm working for a private detective or what, but Mr. Sertant doesn't ever tell me what he does. I just sit here in case anyone comes. Who shall I say is calling, sir?"

"Mr. Barwan, Tedor Barwan."

"Umm." The girl said nothing, but she scowled while trying to write Tedor's name on a pad.

"T-e-d-o-r-space-B-a-r-w-a-n," he spelled it out for her.

"Are you Turkish, Mr. Barwan? It sounds maybe like its Turkish."

"No."

"Mr. Sertant has a funny name, too, Sertant. Excuse me please, Mister."

"That's all right."

"I'd better tell Mr. Sertant you are here." She flicked the intercom, and Tedor could hear a buzzer dimly in the inner office. "Mr. Sertant? There's a Mr. Tedor Barwan to see you. Yes, sir. You go right on in, Mr. Barwan."

TEDOR thanked her, pushed through the gate, opened the door to Sertant's office, and closed it behind him. Sertant got up from his desk, an Agent somewhat younger than Tedor, with red hair and very fair, almost livid skin.

"Your identification please, Barwan."

Tedor gave his papers to Sertant.

"Excellent. It's quite a coincidence you dropped in, Barwan. We've been looking for you."

"Really?"

"It will save us a lot of work."

Tedor was about to ask why, but Sertant began answering the question before he had the opportunity to ask it. Sertant reached into a draw of his desk, his hand emerging swiftly and with clear purpose, grasping a 20th century automatic pistol with comfortable familiarity and pointing it at Tedor.

"Sit down, Barwan."

Tedor sat.

"You're under arrest."

"This is crazy," Tedor snorted, "What for? By what authority? I think I outrank you as an Agent, anyway."

"I don't doubt you do."

"Then you can't arrest me."

"This gun says I can. I also have orders which say I can." With his free hand Sertant groped about the top of his desk, never letting his eyes leave Tedor. Presently he found a sheet of paper tucked under his blotter, passed it across the desk-top.

Tedor scanned it quickly, and with mounting incredulity. It proclaimed:

HEADQUARTERS
CENTURY AGENTS
OFFICE OF THE CHIEF

To all Agents, all centuries: Important. Century Agent C-20 Tedor Barwan—now on vacation, whenabouts unknown—is to be detained on sight for possible connection with or knowledge of serious case of time tinkering.

Signed, Mulid Ruscar, Chief.

"It's Ruscar's signature," said Tedor, "but I still say you can't hold me."

"This gun says I can," Sertant repeated. "I'm sorry, Barwan, but those are my orders. I hardly know anything about it myself, although something seems to be popping right here in this century."

Tedor began to think of getting away. It was something to think about, but not at the moment, for Sertant seemed on the point of telling him something that might be of value.

"Ruscar is here, right here in Twenty. It appears whatever is happening is sufficiently important to demand his presence."

"Well, then, what's happening?"

"My friend, that is what Ruscar will want to ask you. Actually, I don't know. So I'll simply have to detain you until Ruscar gets here—which could be soon. It could also be several weeks."

Tedor did not like the idea of an indefinite wait. He eyed Sertant speculatively wondered just how much experience the young Agent had with the obsolete pistol—how much he had, in fact with violence of any sort.

Tedor calculated the distance between them. Six feet, with Sertant sitting comfortably behind the desk, elbow propped on its surface, gun in hand; Tedor standing in front of the desk, shifting his weight uncomfortably from one foot to the other.

The desk? Tedor considered. It wasn't too heavy, but it also did not give him much of a handhold. If he could duck, grasp it firmly, spill it over on top of Sertant...

Sertant settled the problem himself. He stood up, came around the side of the desk and stopped near Tedor. "I really should put this antique weapon away," he admitted. "After all, we Agents can trust one another, and Ruscar probably wants you only for information on something."

Tedor shrugged, beginning to feel like a heel, but realizing it was necessary. "Then why don't you?"

SERTANT looked at the gun uncertainly; but continued holding it, the muzzle pointed half at Tedor and half at the floor. "You are going to be a headache," he said. "Obviously, I can't lock you in any of the 20th century jails. The natives would want reasons and I don't have the authority, anyway."

"Then why don't you let me go—provided I promise to remain in the 20th century until I see Ruscar?" Tedor realized he could cheerfully make such a promise and keep it, for if they uncovered and defeated the monopolist in Russia, Ruscar assuredly would want to hear of it.

Sertant shook his head, "Since Ruscar issued this directive for you personally, I have to detain you."

At that moment, Sertant's office intercom buzzed. Sertant leaned across the desk, his eyes still on Tedor, and flicked a switch. Tedor heard the secretary's voice.

"Mr. Sertant, I'd like to see you about something."

"What?" Sertant demanded irritably.

"Your correspondence to Mr. Hoblan in Cairo."

Hoblan's name was familiar to Tedor. C-20, middle-east, as he recalled.

"Umm, yes. That can't wait. Come on in, Miss Peterson."

The door soon opened. Sertant averted his eyes from Tedor for an instant, looked at Miss Peterson.

Tedor leaped at him. The gun roared deafeningly, brought a cascade of plaster down from the ceiling, Miss Peterson screamed.

Then Tedor was grappling with Sertant, forcing him back over the edge of the desk, and twisting the hand that held the gun. Miss Peterson disappeared, on her way to notify the local police in all probability.

Tedor twisted savagely, heard something snap. Sertant cursed; the gun clattered to the desk-top, then to the floor, but Sertant's hand was at Tedor's throat, choking him. Abruptly Tedor relaxed, permitting Sertant to straighten away from the desk. Tedor swung his right hand in a short clubbing blow, which chopped at Sertant's chin. It broke Sertant's choking hold, opened Sertant's guard so Tedor could pound two swift blows at his stomach.

Sertant doubled over, got thrust upright again by a hard left cross which loosened his teeth and sent two of them flying from his mouth with a spray of blood. Sertant gurgled, covered head with hands and slumped on the desk.

Tedor left the office, tidying his clothing. In the outer room he passed a near-hysterical Miss Peterson, who had just returned the phone to its cradle.

"Better get him some water," Tedor told her. "Cold water. And tell him I'm sorry. Tell him I'm an Agent, doing an Agent's job and nothing, not even Ruscar, can delay it. Tell him Ruscar can find me in Moscow if he really wants me."

"M-Moscow?"

"Moscow." Tedor closed the door behind him.

CHAPTER TWELVE

DORLUP was sweating. Naturally, he had nothing to hide; he had done nothing which could call the Agents down on him. "I don't know what you're talking about," he repeated for the fifth time.

"We'll see about that. We have a sworn statement by this solidio actress—"

"Beti? That's insane. Beti's been with me for months, I admit that; but my behavior has always been within the limits of the law. Why man, the natives accept me as one of their own."

"That's what you say."

"Yes it is, I challenge you to prove otherwise."

"We already have. The actress' testimony is enough to condemn you."

"I demand that my legal advocate be notified."

"He will, when you're returned to the future for trial."

The door to the small room opened. Tall, slender, self-assured, Mulid Ruscar entered with another man.

"It's done," the other man said.

"We have her statement," said Ruscar. "You can send this one back any time—and just a minute! Something's coming over your teletype. This primitive communications…"

The man who had been questioning Dorlup walked to a bulky piece of machinery, which was clicking excitedly in a corner of the room. He peered in through the metal case, read:

HEADQUARTERS EASTERN UNITED STATES DISTRICT COLON URGENT EXCLAMATION POINT IS RUSCAR PRESENT QUESTION PLEASE HAVE HIM CONTACT ME IMMEDIATELY REGARDING TEDOR BARWAN PERIOD BARWAN WAS HERE BUT MAN-AGED TO ESCAPE CMM TRICKING AND OVERPOWERING ME PERIOD BARWAN ASSERTED INTENTIONS OF VISITING MOSCOW USSR CMM PURPOSE OF VISIT UNKNOWN PERIOD PLEASE

NOTIFY PERIOD JELDON SERTANT C TWENTY
NEUSA CMM NEW YORK NY END

"Barwan's slipped through our fingers again," the man
said bitterly.

Ruscar frowned at him. "Actually, you're jumping to
conclusions concerning Tedor. He's a good man, one of the
best Agents we've got."

"That's just it, Chief. That's exactly it. He's been so well
indoctrinated in Agenting, he'll never play along with us."

"No. Who do you think it was who indoctrinated Tedor?
I did, I believed that way myself, you know. If I changed my
mind, perhaps I can change Tedor's. I'd certainly like to,
because we can use Tedor.

"Well, you can take this Dorlup thing from here. The girl
has had an unfortunate accident. She's dead. But we have
her statement, and it should hold up in a court of law."

"Dead!" Dorlup cried, not understanding what was going
on.

"Take him out of here," Ruscar said, and someone
removed Dorlup from the room.

"Now, then," Ruscar continued. "Return to our century
with him. Press charges. Make an astonishing revelation, as
it were. We doubted the existence of a monopolist of
despotism, but we're not infallible. We were wrong. Dorlup
is the monopolist, and we have proof."

"Poor Dorlup."

"One of those things. We needed a scapegoat, because
too many people were beginning to demand action regarding
Domique Hadrien's claims. Too bad we couldn't stick it on
Hadrien himself; that would be taking care of two things at
once.

"About Barwan, tell Sertant to forget it. If Barwan's on
his way to Moscow, then we can only assume he's thrown in
completely with Domique Hadrien and his followers. That

doesn't mean it's irrevocable, for I'm going to Moscow myself. I'd like to have Barwan with us, as you know. If not—well, no one man is indispensable."

In the next room, meanwhile, Dorlup was fuming. His whole orientation toward what had happened had been drastically altered in the last few moments. It was not a mistake, hardly a mistake at all.

A plot?

A plot, decidedly. Dorlup was being used as—what was the 20th century term he had picked up?—as a fall guy. He'd have none of it. Not Dorlup. At first he hardly knew how to straighten it out, but if Ruscar wouldn't help—he had counted on Ruscar and now it seemed Ruscar was behind everything—then Dorlup had only one place to turn. He smiled grimly. After what had happened at the Eradrome, he never thought he'd go to Tedor Barwan for anything.

The guard kept one eye on Dorlup, and at the same time tried to listen, through a partially opened door to the conservation in the next room. Dorlup picked up a chair when he was convinced all the guard's attentions were centered on the other room. He swung the chair like a four-stemmed club, shattering it over the guard's head. Feet pounded in the next room, but Dorlup was on his way out.

Shots barked in the darkness, and once a parabeam zipped past Dorlup. But he kept on running and he found a car at the head of the driveway. Not only were the keys in the ignition, the engine was idling. Dorlup sprung inside for all his massive bulk and had gunned the automobile out toward the main highway before another car started in pursuit.

Heading for the road to Reno and his time-conveyor, Dorlup wondered how he could approach Tedor Barwan in Moscow—if, indeed Tedor was on his way there. Well, Dorlup knew a man in the Spasso House, the American Embassy fronting on Red Square. He was an expatriate time-traveler who had decided to remain in the 20th century as one of its citizens—something growing more common every day. Perhaps he could help Dorlup...

If he ever got to his time-conveyor, let alone Moscow.

Headlights blazed in his rearview mirror. He pressed his right foot down on the accelerator, as far as it would go. The lights did not fade, nor did they grow brighter.

CHAPTER THIRTEEN

"IT can't really be him," Georgi Malenkov told the Comrade Doctor in obvious distaste.

"I assure you, Comrade Premier it is he."

Malenkov walked ponderously to a bar in the corner, poured himself two ounces of vodka and drank them straight. His suite was far within the walls of the Kremlin, so deep and so well hidden, in fact, that not fifty people in all of Moscow knew its location. For Stalin this had not been necessary, Malenkov thought uncomfortably. His suite had been secret, true enough—but thousands of people had known its location. With Malenkov it was different. He could trust no one—no one. He never knew a man could feel so completely alone, so helpless at night and afraid to sleep. Every time he saw Vladimir Chenkov's lean, gaunt face he went almost sick with fear.

Chenkov, grim, deadly Chief of Staff of the Red Army, who had arisen from Ural obscurity to power only this year— Chenkov coveted what he did.

Not Chenkov alone. Everyone. Why, he couldn't even trust his servants—two men and a woman who never saw the light of day, never ventured from his suite in the Kremlin.

He was not Stalin, not the Iron Man, not the half-deity. He was Malenkov, the man, the fat half-Tartar—and afraid. He had thought at first that in a matter of months he could cement his position securely enough to venture forth without fear. But here it was, more than a year and a half since he had taken office and he had still to drive along the private Highway and use his private dacha to the south for a few days of relaxation.

Fortified with the vodka, Malenkov scowled at the Comrade Doctor. "I won't ask you to explain—such explanations are beyond me. You say it is he. Very well, but hear this: if you are lying, if you are wrong—lying or not—your life shall be forfeit."

The Comrade Doctor shrugged. "I spoke the truth."

Everyone was against him, Malenkov sulked. Everyone. Now even a ghost. "How long will he live—uh, he *is* living?"

"The answer to the second question, Comrade Premier, is yes. He is alive, although the manner of life is decidedly unusual. As for the first question, does the Premier want a truthful answer?"

"I insist upon it," said Malenkov, who now desired more vodka, but thought it a matter of impropriety to return to the bar and so call the Comrade Doctor's attention to the fact that he drank heavily. Such things had a way of getting out and causing trouble. Perhaps Chenkov would know some way to use it as a weapon.

"Then, I do not know. I can promise nothing. He is alive now—in a very special sort of way. How long he will live I cannot predict. He might die in a minute, an hour, a year— he might live, if properly cared for, for an eternity. He—"

The phone buzzed. Malenkov shuddered, jumped. It had sounded so loud. He must have them mute the phones.

"This is the Comrade Premier," he said.

"Comrade Zhubin, the bio-chemist, Comrade Premier."

Zhubin. Malenkov's heart pounded. "Go ahead Zhubin."

"He is calling for you."

"Already?" Malenkov was hoarse, found it difficult to swallow. "How long has he been calling for me?"

"Several minutes. He is laughing as if something is quite funny."

Malenkov said he would be right there, returned the phone to its hook. He shuddered again. The thought of the thing in its small round glass case was terrible. Should he tell the people? Already rumors were afoot. Who couldn't he trust? The Comrade Doctor. Shuddering was becoming habitual. He *had* to trust the Comrade Doctor, or die of fright every time he got the sniffles. The Comrade biochemist, Zhubin? But Zhubin had the thing in the glass case and might be considered the second most important man in the Communist hierarchy.

Then who was first?

Malenkov?

The thing in the glass case?

Shuddering Malenkov bid the Comrade Doctor make himself comfortable. He excused himself, entered the hall and started walking. Who was first? He suddenly remembered something, Malenkov was not first, nor was the thing in the case. Someone else—someone none of the Russians knew anything about, except for Malenkov, and Stalin before him, and perhaps one or two others.

But Mulid Ruscar, the quiet man impossibly (and yet it was so) from the future, preferred to remain in the background.

After all, hadn't the thing in the glass case been Ruscar's idea?

CHAPTER FOURTEEN

"BUT of course, Vladimir, my dear—of course I missed you! Could it be otherwise, ever?"

Laniq sat curled on a chair, talking into the telephone. Her transformation had been amazing, thought Tedor. Not many hours before, they had set their conveyor down a score of miles south of Moscow, in a heavily wooded area. Dressed like city folk and equipped with all the counterfeit documents they needed, they had confiscated an auto (Laniq's forged paper placed them high in the Communist nobility) and motored to Moscow.

There they entered the apartment Laniq maintained. Laniq excused herself, left Tedor in the living room with some good vodka, and went into the bedroom to change her clothing.

Tedor had to whistle when she returned.

The gown clung to her body, dazzling white, patterned with gems, slashed boldly from throat to waist revealing Laniq's shapely breasts as much as it concealed them, revealing and concealing in a breathless rhythm as she moved about. The skirt also was slit on one side to mid-thigh.

"I'm going to call Chenkov and have dinner with him," Laniq had said. "Find out what's going on."

For answer, Tedor took her in his arms and kissed her. It was one of those things, a sudden impulse, which he regretted, in the first split second. Regret turned to delight. Laniq seemed surprised, tried to pull away, but all at once her lips melted under his, her arms were flung about his neck, her body thrust against him.

"Laniq," he had murmured. "Laniq, I—"

"Shh!" And they were kissing again.

"Laniq—it's crazy, wild, impossible. We hardly know each other, we…I came into time looking for you wanting to kill you!"

"We have been through all of civilization together. I know you for five thousand years. Umm-mm, don't stop, Tedor."

And he hadn't, not for a long time. She burned like fire and she cooled like a clear mountain lake on a hot summer day and Tedor had whispered in the dark, "I love you, Laniq."

"Tedor! I love you. Tell me again."

"I love you."

And afterwards, he had prepared drinks and they toasted the future and discussed plans and then Laniq had gone to the telephone and called Chenkov.

"I have to see you, Vladimir. I missed you every minute." Tedor stood nearby; she kissed the tip of his nose.

Tedor was so close he heard the voice faintly over the receiver. "I'm busy, but I'll put it aside. Dinner and then my dacha for the night, darling Anna."

That was Laniq's name here in Russia, Anna Myinkov. As Anna Myinkov she had on previous visits captivated the hearts of Chenkov and others. Only fat Georgi Malenkov, she had told Tedor, had been impossibly aloof. Of course, the extent of her captivation was information. She could learn what was happening, but Tedor somehow would have to put it to use.

"I'll pick you up in an hour, Anna."

"An hour, then," and Laniq cut the connection, turning into Tedor's arms.

Tedor scowled. "Just what happens at his dacha?"

Laniq laughed softly, "Silly Tedor, we're not married yet." But her eyes were twinkling.

"What happens?"

"You leave that to me, but I can tell you this: if I gave Chenkov what he could get, and gladly, from any Russian beauty, he'd tire of me."

"Just what do you do?"

Laniq practiced some exaggerated bumps and grinds like those Tedor had often seen in the Eradrome. "Enough, but not too much. Listen, Tedor—you'd better be on your way in a few minutes. What happens if Chenkov finds you here?"

Grumbling, Tedor picked up his fur-lined coat and Russian pile-cap. "There's a man at the Spasso House," he told her. "Someone who decided he liked the twentieth century better than our own, counterfeited a birth certificate, deposited it in an American department of health some thirty years ago and took up citizenship there. He went into state department work and is here in Moscow now.

"You get what information you can from Chenkov. I'll see my friend. We'll compare notes and decide what to do. Laniq—I want you to—well, be careful, that's all."

"Well..." Laniq smiled at him.

"I'm not joking. Maybe that gown kind of hurried what I felt all along, but it was coming, Laniq. I loved you from the beginning but didn't know it. Laniq, be careful."

"You can come back and sleep here tonight if you want. I'll see you in the morning. And you know I'll be careful, Tedor. Now that I've found you I want to keep you—and I want to stay healthy enough to appreciate what I've got."

The phone rang.

"Hello, this is Anna Myinkov.

Yes? Oh, yes, Vladimir. My, but that was fast. Of course." Laniq hung up, shoved Tedor toward the door. "Get out of here, quick! Chenkov's suite of rooms when he's not in the Kremlin or his dacha is in a hotel down the street. He's early. He's on his way up right now. Scram!"

Tedor kissed her quickly, stalked out into the hall and waited for the elevator. A middle-aged man got off—wearing the uniform of a Red Army marshal, carrying a large bouquet of flowers.

"You should have doffed your hat," the female elevator operator admonished Tedor as they started down. "That was Marshal Chenkov."

"Don't I know it," said Tedor.

"BARWAN! This is a surprise. Come in, come in."

The Spasso House, the American Embassy adjacent to Red Square, was a gaunt, grim structure. Frawdin Chlon—Harry Marsden now—was a man of about Tedor's age, but shorter, fair of skin and hair and quite calm and self-possessed in an American business suit.

"We were about to close for the day, Barwan. But this is a surprise."

"How are you, Frawdin—no, I guess it had better be Harry."

"You're telling me! Fine, thank you. It's quite a coincidence, because I had another visitor earlier today. He says he knows you and wanted to see you, but I had no idea you were in Moscow."

"Who was that?"

"A solidio writer, name of Dorlup."

"Dorlup?" Tedor frowned.

"He claims to be in some kind of trouble and says he has a story to tell which would make your hair stand on end."

"He has a habit of doing that. Do you have his address?"

Marsden nodded, then asked: "What brings you here?"

"It's a long story, and since you are working for the American government now, I don't think I'd better tell you. Not that anything I plan doing will hurt America—far from it. But you know about time-travel and the way we have to do everything in secret. All I want is some information, anyway. What's the current international state of affairs?"

"I wish I knew, Tedor. Frankly, I'm worried. The Russians have massed three million troops on their European border, another million to the east, north of the Yellow Sea. Their big planes, capable of delivering anything including atomic weapons a third of the way around the world, are lined up on a 'round-the-clock stand-by basis at half a dozen airfields; there's talk they'll be used soon. Everything seems to hinge on something happening in the Kremlin right now. There's talk, wild rumors, but nothing official."

"What are the rumors about?"

"You'll think this is silly, but they're from usually reliable sources. They claim Stalin has come back to life."

"What!"

"That's right. Stalin has come back, sort of like a totalitarian Communist Messiah. All people have a culture-hero who's supposed to come back in times of trouble and lead his nation to glory. Even though Stalin's been gone only a year and a half, he's the Russian culture-hero. If somehow they can rig up a setup—the men in the Kremlin, I mean—which convinces the people he has come back and wants war, there's no telling what Russia might do."

"But does the Kremlin want war?"

Marsden shrugged, "It might be necessary to keep power. The people don't like their government, although they tolerated it under Stalin because he managed to convince them he was something of a deity. But if the government can turn the people to an exterior trouble, namely a world war, the government would stay in power. It depends on what these rumors are all about."

"And don't you know?"

"No."

"Okay, Harry. Thanks. Listen, don't tell Dorlup I was here if he should call you, I'll get in touch with him when I have a chance."

Marsden gave Tedor an address where Dorlup could be reached, told him they'd have to have lunch together some time, then led him to the door.

VLADIMIR Chenkov's dacha—his big estate at the far end of the private highway some thirty-odd miles south of Moscow, almost had the proportions of a palace. It was big all over, with huge rooms, high ceilings, half a dozen fireplaces, two grand pianos, ponderous, overstuffed furniture and eight private bedrooms, each easily large enough to accommodate four people although each contained only one oversized bed.

"You're a strange girl, Anna," said Chenkov, sitting with her on bearskins near the fireplace and trying to maneuver in such a way that when she grew tired her head would naturally fall into his lap.

"Oh, I like you—yes. Don't misunderstand. But at times you are so—cold."

"You're married, Vladimir, and sometimes I think of your wife and think of how I would feel under similar circumstances."

"That is all?"

"Well—"

"Then listen to me, Anna. What is a wife? A man has a wife because it is conventional, like a country says it is striving for peace when often it must have war to keep from flying apart. I can get you anything, anything. I could treat you like no wife ever was treated. Here, you like this dacha? Say the word and it is yours."

Servants came with vodka, champagne, paper-thin slices of sturgeon, caviar. Chenkov nibbled at the sturgeon while Laniq had some caviar and champagne. Chenkov began drinking vodka and hardly paused until, Laniq realized, he was high enough to be uninhibited, yet not sufficiently high to be a boor. It was the gentlemanly thing in Russian nobility, Laniq knew.

"Do you not even feel inclined to kiss me tonight, my Anna?"

Laniq offered her lips without heat, got them bruised by Chenkov's teeth.

"Then at least dance for me, Anna."

She had danced for him before, here in this very dacha, at the same fireplace. But now it was different, now she could not feel the same emotional indifference and so whet Chenkov's appetite sufficiently for him to start talking.

Laniq got up and did a tentative pirouette.

"Come now."

Laniq danced slowly, spinning and dipping and feeling terribly sorry for herself. But the firelight was warm and the champagne, and the whole room seemed to go out of focus except for Chenkov's hungry eyes, which became enormous—and in Laniq's own time the dance was something to be done because you loved doing it, and except for Chenkov's eyes she might dance with abandon and enjoy herself.

Tedor, she thought. *Tedor...*

IF she closed her own eyes she thought, almost, she was dancing for him and not for Chenkov. The slit skirt swirled around her flashing thighs; the bodice, slashed from throat to waist, clung and fell away, clung and fell away.

She danced not for Chenkov but for Tedor—and then not for Tedor but for all the people in the world who might live in freedom if Chenkov's tongue loosened. But the hands, which reached up for her legs and pulled her down, were Chenkov's.

"Tell me," she said breathlessly while Chenkov tried to paw her and she scampered away to fill a large glass with vodka for him and a small one with champagne for herself. "Tell me, are you as important a man as I hear?"

"My dear Anna! You're jesting."

"No I mean it. I'm only a country girl, really I am, and I'd—"

"You? A country bumpkin. That's good, that's splendid. Well, then I will tell you. I am number two man in all the realm, and…"

Laniq pouted.

"Don't cry. Don't. I will one day be number one man. I know it. You may rest assured of that. I could show you things, so many things which would make your beautiful hair stand on end."

"Then show me!"

"Very well—I shall, my Anna."

"Show me how you can do anything, anything you want in all of Moscow."

"And in the Kremlin, too," Chenkov said thickly. "Yes, in the Kremlin. Tomorrow morning I will take you to see something you never dreamed of. Tomorrow morning…" He kissed her wetly, too far gone with vodka.

"Tomorrow morning then, I'm sleepy." And Laniq stood up, brushed his fumbling hands away from her, climbed the stairs to the second floor, retreated to a bedroom and bolted the door behind her. Chenkov was soon stomping up the stairs and banging insistently at the door.

"Tomorrow," Laniq whispered, and repeated it when Chenkov protested, "I said tomorrow."

"But Anna—"

"You show me what you can do. After all, I don't want to be a fly-by-night mistress of this dacha. Good night, Vladimir."

"Good night, then. Tomorrow morning—and tomorrow night."

THEY always tried to bring Chenkov in on everything. *They* actually had more power than people on the outside could imagine, Malenkov thought petulantly. They numbered only two-score but they were his cabinet of ministers and sub-ministers and it seemed—ridiculously—that he had to answer to them for everything, "But why don't we forget about Vladimir?" Malenkov pleaded, "who must certainly be kept busy with his Army work?"

"Vladimir will come. Stalin would have wanted it that way."

Stalin, in truth, had asked for Chenkov as well as Malenkov. Stalin. Malenkov trembled when he thought of it. That was not Stalin—that was nobody. A thing, not a person. It spoke even with a mechanical voice. Stalin—the Old Stalin—never answered to a cabinet of ministers and sub-ministers.

As for the new Stalin, the strange horrible thing which the biochemist, Zhubin, insisted was Stalin, there was no telling what he would want or demand. Malenkov wished passionately he could get his hands around Zhubin's scrawny neck and choke the life from him. This was all Zhubin's fault.

Not really, for Mulid Ruscar couldn't be discounted. Why did everything happen this way? Why did men from the future even insist on poking their noses into his, Malenkov's business? But why was any of this Ruscar's affair, anyway? Ruscar seemed to hold the whip hand. Ruscar told them what to do, and they did it. Ruscar knew political intrigue as well as a Chenkov, bio-chemistry as well as a Zhubin—for was it not Ruscar who had helped, paved the way, in fact, for Zhubin to construct the monster masquerading as a resurrected Stalin? As if a hideous, naked thing in a glass cage could be a man of flesh and blood and think like a man.

"Hurry, Comrade Premier. Ruscar is waiting and Stalin with him."

Ruscar—and Stalin. But Ruscar had not been born yet, and would not be, for thousands of years. Stalin? Stalin was dead.

"I do not feel well," said Malenkov. "Summon the Comrade Doctor."

"I am here, Comrade Premier. I will go with you to the meeting. A slight sedative will perhaps—"

"No! Get that thing away from me!" Malenkov recoiled in terror from the needle which the Comrade Doctor had extended. "I am all right."

Was the Comrade Doctor in the employ of Chenkov to poison him? Was he in the employ of Ruscar for some nameless purpose? Or of Zhubin, the bio-chemist, to transform Malenkov also into a pink thing floating in ghastly fluid in a little glass container?

Almost blubbering as he walked toward the laboratory, Malenkov could feel the weight of Communist Empire crushing him like a worm to the floor.

"I've never been in the Kremlin," Laniq told Chenkov as they hurried along the silent hallways within the walled fortress. She had seen the towers, the minarets, the gaunt walls only briefly from the outside, and then Chenkov had spirited her within the place, although clearly a Red Army guard would have protested had he been anyone but the Chief of Staff.

"I can take you anywhere you want," Chenkov promised, walking beside her, his arm tucked in hers, resembling neither the whip-lash leader of the Army, which he was, nor the romantic lover, which he hoped to be—but rather the obscure military figure who had climbed to glory over the purge-slain bodies of his comrades. He would one day look the part of the field marshal, Laniq thought; at the moment he was trying to convince himself as well as Anna Myinkov of the brightness of his star in the communist firmament.

They reached a heavy metal door flanked by two guards. "Marshal Chenkov!" cried one, and they both saluted with their rifles. The door opened, they went inside.

CHAPTER FIFTEEN

LANIQ saw a huge room, a laboratory it seemed—all white porcelain and gleaming chrome. At the far end a group of men clustered about an object, which seemed suspended in air and bathed in radiance of gold and amber. The object was cylindrical and rather small, transparent with a pinkish mass floating inside.

Laniq almost screamed. The thing in the glass container was a human brain.

Chenkov grasped her arm more tightly. "They won't like it when they find I brought you here." He smiled. "They'll probably insist you remain within the Kremlin—with me."

A big, nervous man with flabby jowls and the palest face Laniq had ever seen turned to face them.

"Vladimir," he said, "you're late."

It was Georgi Malenkov.

Chenkov shrugged. "I am here."

"And your friend?"

"She is that, a friend."

"You shouldn't have brought her. What do you think this is, a circus?"

"It's a private affair. She's harmless."

"I'll summon the guards and have her removed."

"Yes? To whom do you think the guards owe their first allegiance?"

A white-smocked figure turned to look at the newcomers. "Please, Comrades. Let's have none of this squabbling, Stalin wants to talk with us."

"We'll settle this later," grumbled Malenkov.

"There is nothing to settle," said Chenkov, standing his ground.

Malenkov growled, but looked again at the brain floating in its case. The white-smocked figure adjusted some dials on a table nearby. On the wall behind the glass enclosed brain, a microphone speaker blared metallically: "Are they both here? Malenkov and Chenkov, both of them?"

"Yes," said Zhubin. "Yes, Comrade Stalin. They are here."

"You now know that I live," said the brain. "It is a strange new life I have, but I can think—perhaps more clearly than would otherwise be possible, for I have no body to encumber me. Before I go on, do you have any questions?"

Malenkov blinked his fat-enveloped eyes. Chenkov stared.

"Very well. The day my body died, a quick operation removed the brain and preserved it. Comrade Zhubin— working under the direction of a man you've only seen once or twice—transferred the brain, my brain exactly as it was in life so that when I speak you will know it is Stalin, the Man of Iron, talking into this case. I have since conferred with the man who made the operation possible, the man who can do great things for Mother Russia, and because talking tires me in some strange way and he knows the situation more completely at this time than I do. I want you to listen to him as if it were I, Stalin, talking."

There was a silence. The half dozen figures still stood around the brain case, but one of them turned slowly around to look at all the earnest faces. His eyes raked Laniq, "A woman?" he said, incredulously, and his eyes wandered, then darted back. "Laniq Hadrien!" he cried. "Who brought this woman here? Fools! Speak!"

"It was Chenkov," fat Malenkov said spitefully.

"Is that true?" the man demanded.

Chenkov nodded defiantly. "So what?"

"So what? So this, you idiot! That girl is a representative of our most dangerous enemy."

"The United States?" wailed Malenkov.

"Far worse than the United States."

Laniq sprinted for the doorway at the other end of the room, heard the voice call from behind her: "Guards! Stop that woman!"

The speaker was Mulid Ruscar.

WHEN Laniq failed to return Tedor began to worry. It suddenly occurred to him that he might be able to reach Mulid Ruscar for help. True, Ruscar had sent out an order for his arrest, but directives could be mis-read, transferred incorrectly. Perhaps Ruscar merely needed him urgently. Perhaps Ruscar had realized he would be flitting through the ages and nothing short of arrest would detain him long enough for them to get together. Tedor used his tongue to flick on the tiny transmitter embedded in his palate, then said:

"This is Tedor Barwan calling Mulid Ruscar. Barwan calling Ruscar!"

He waited not more than half a minute when the answering voice whispered in his ear. "Tedor, where are you?"

"In Moscow, Chief. I'm sorry I couldn't wait in New York. I have news for you. It's about Laniq Hadrien."

"Laniq? Oh, of course, Laniq Hadrien eh? Where are you?"

Tedor gave Ruscar his address.

"Fine, Tedor, I'll send someone over to fetch you. Stay right there."

"All right, chief." And Tedor cut the connection. Ruscar had a way about him for getting to the bottom of intrigue. Tedor felt better already.

A moment later, the doorbell rang. Ruscar's man? Impossible.

Tedor opened the door and admitted a nervous Dorlup.

"Barwan, thank heaven I found you. Harry Marsden gave me your address."

Tedor watched guardedly, as Dorlup entered the room, sat down on a big chair. "Have you people got any closer to finding the time tyrant?"

Tedor shook his head.

"Let me ask you another question. At the very beginning of all this you were going to write a report. What was it about?"

"The 20th century, of course. I was going to say it seemed that the most aggressive, war-like state here, Russia, was receiving aid from our own time. Fornswitthe started to write it."

"That's what I thought." Dorlup mopped his forehead, although it was comfortably warm in the apartment. "And someone killed him and stole it. You thought I was the only one who could have known where Fornswitthe was living. But someone else knew, Mulid Ruscar knew."

"Of course Ruscar knew," Tedor declared irritably. "That doesn't mean anything. Ruscar is fighting everything the monopolist stands for."

"We'll get back to that. It might interest you to know I'm a fugitive. I escaped from Ruscar in the United States when Ruscar accused me of being the time tyrant."

"I've wondered the same thing myself. But somehow you don't fill the role."

"He has enough phony evidence to make it stick, Barwan. You see, certain people were creating too much of a fuss about the monopolist. It was crimping Ruscar's plans. He figured if he could convict a scapegoat the furor would die down, at least for a while. I was his scapegoat."

Tedor frowned while he poured them both drinks. "It just doesn't make sense. Ruscar all his life has stood for everything the monopolist was trying to tear down.

"Which is exactly why no one ever suspected him."

"I think you're crazy, or lying, or wrong—but we'll find out soon enough. Ruscar knows I'm in Moscow. He's sending someone over, as it matter of fact."

"If Ruscar is sending someone to find you we've got to get out of here!" Dorlup gasped.

"Calm down. We'll do no such thing. We'll wait for Ruscar's man and see what this is all about."

"*You'll* wait, you mean—if you are stupid enough to aid in your own execution. I'm getting out of here." Dorlup climbed to his feet, but Tedor pushed him back into his chair.

"You're waiting with me, Dorlup. I'd like to find out once and for all just where you fit into all this."

"Barwan, I came to you in good faith! Give me a chance! Ruscar has enough rigged evidence to have me gassed."

"Sit still and wait."

Dorlup emptied his glass of vodka, reached over to the table and tremblingly poured another.

Seconds later the doorbell rang.

HE was tall, broad of shoulder, wore a snap-brim hat and a concealed weapon which nevertheless bulged on his hip. He showed his credentials. "I am from Army Intelligence," he announced. "The Chief of Staff's Office instructed me personally to escort you to a meeting with a Comrade Ruscar."

"Chief of Staff," said Dorlup. "That would be Chenkov himself. You're a big fish, Barwan."

Tedor wondered if there could be any truth in all that Dorlup had said. Looking at Dorlup now, he realized the man bordered on hysteria, and even if he were indeed well-meaning, he could still have misinterpreted everything. Unlikely—but no less likely than the accusations Dorlup had made against Mulid Ruscar. Perhaps the Intelligence Agent could inadvertently shed light on the entire situation.

Tedor yawned, "I am tired. I think I have changed my mind. Yes, I'd rather sleep. You tell the Chief of Staff to tell Ruscar I won't see him today, after all."

"But Comrade, I was sent to get you."

"Fine, you're a good man. I'm sending you back without me. Care for a drink before you leave?"

"Thank you, no. I never drink on duty. Comrade, listen; the Chief of Staff would hate to tell Comrade Ruscar that you have changed your mind, I know this for a fact, Comrade."

"Are you trying to say I haven't much choice? I go with you voluntarily or get taken?"

The Intelligence Agent shrugged, "I never said it and you are putting it crudely, even coarsely. But the general assumption is correct."

Still smiling, Tedor reached for the bottle of vodka, which stood on a table near the door. The Intelligence Agent stood with one foot inside the apartment, one outside, waiting.

"Go to hell," said Tedor.

The Intelligence Agent reached quickly for his gun. Tedor swung the vodka bottle in a short, savage arc at the right side of the man's face while he fumbled in his pocket for the weapon. The bottle struck his jawbone, shattered. He screamed and fell, his face a red smear.

Tedor dragged him inside the apartment and shut the door. "Maybe you know what you're talking about, Dorlup. Are you willing to help me prove it?"

"I guess so. Yes, of course!"

Tedor reached into the fallen Intelligence Agent's pocket, found his wallet, his identification card with a picture and his gun. "We'll need this," he said. "Come on."

Laniq's commandeered auto was still parked at the curb downstairs, a crowd of urchins admiring it. "Climb in," Tedor told Dorlup, then walked to a display board down the street, found a poster with Malenkov's picture, quickly removed it and ran for the car. "We're dead ducks if my time conveyor isn't where I left it," he said. "If it's there, we may have a chance."

AND half an hour later: "So we're in your conveyor. Now what?"

"Sit down," said Tedor. "We've got to hurry."

"But this is the matter duplicator."

Tedor nodded. Each conveyor was equipped with one of the devices—which could print perfect counterfeit money, create clothing, artificial hair, skin tissue, anything to render a visit to past ages as foolproof as possible.

"Whatever you want to copy is ordinarily stored on microfilm," Tedor explained. "But this thing can copy anything."

"I know, but what do you want me—"

Tedor thrust the picture of Malenkov into the receiver. "Easy, Dorlup. You're about the right size. Just sit still. You're going to be Georgi Malenkov, Premier of all the Russians."

Five minutes later, Tedor looked at Malenkov rising from the chair. "It's perfect," he said.

"I don't understand."

"You can write solidios, Dorlup; you'd better be able to *act* as well. You're going to be Malenkov."

Tedor sat down himself, placed the Intelligence Agent's ID picture into the duplicator. "I'll be your personal bodyguard," he said—and he was, moments later.

"They've got a friend of mine somewhere," said Tedor. "If Chenkov takes orders from Malenkov, we're going to find out where. We're also going to find out what Ruscar has up his sleeve, provided you're right about him."

"I'm right."

"We'll see. But if you were lying, Dorlup—if you were, I'll kill you myself."

Dorlup blanched. "We don't have to worry about that."

"All right. According to his ID card, this man was Fyodor Archevski. I'm Fyodor Archevski, your guard."

And then they were speeding in Laniq's auto back to Moscow—and the Kremlin.

"WHERE do you think you are going? Oh, Comrade Premier, Comrade Malenkov—I am sorry."

Dorlup nodded brusquely at the guard. They drove through the Kremlin gates and up a ramp.

"Do you know your way around this place?" Dorlup demanded.

"No."

Tedor stopped the car. They climbed out, watched as a uniformed figure darted out from a doorway, leaped into the auto, drove it away after saluting them.

Another figure came forward. "May I be of help, Comrade Premier?"

"The Premier wishes an immediate audience with Comrade Chenkov," Tedor told the soldier. "Not in his private quarters but in the nearest available study. Lead us to it and have someone fetch Chenkov. Quickly."

The guard took them up another ramp, through a doorway, down a hall. He led them into a spacious sitting room, soon had the fireplace burning brightly. "I'll get the Marshal myself," he said, and departed.

Tedor looked around, discovered a draped alcove at one end of the room. Peering inside he saw a dressing table and a mirror. "I'll be in here," he said. "Remember, the first thing you want to find out from Chenkov is this: where's Laniq? Her name's Anna Myinkov, and Chenkov knows her, probably saw her yesterday and possibly more recently than that. Afterwards, if Chenkov wants to tell you anything in addition, that'll be fine."

A few moments later, Chenkov stalked angrily into the study, "See here, Georgi! I saw you not half an hour ago in your quarters and now you bring me here. What is it?"

Dorlup cleared his throat. "I wanted some information."

"You sound strange."

"Cold coming on, I think, Vladimir, tell me—what happened to the girl? You know, Anna Myinkov?"

"Why should you be interested in her? Anyway, you *know* what happened. Don't tell me the living brain of Stalin frightened you so much you didn't even see what was going on?"

"Y-yes. That was it, Vladimir."

Chenkov snorted, "And the mantle of powers is yours. Well, Ruscar said Anna was from some enemy force and since she was his enemy she was also ours, I had a hard time explaining my way out of that one, but Ruscar must have realized I hold enough power here to give him trouble if he tries to give me some. He probably has Anna in the Lubianka Prison and I intend to do something about it, although why you should be interested, I don't know."

Dorlup was a doleful-looking Malenkov, but the features were identical—the tiny eyes, high forehead, thick jowls, petulant lips. Hiding in the dressing alcove, Tedor wondered how long the ruse would hold.

"I was just curious, that's all."

"It seems to me other things should be on your mind. I'm the Chief of Staff, so it's not my problem. But with Ruscar and Stalin—"

"Stalin? I—"

"Stalin's brain, Georgi. His brain. Ruscar resurrected it, not I. If the war goes badly—it shouldn't, but if it does—the people will have a resurrected Stalin to turn to for faith and hope. It was a stroke of genius, I think. But right now you and Molotov should be conferring with the military leaders, getting things ready, planning..."

"It's arranged," Dorlup said evasively, "It's all arranged."

"So quickly? That's preposterous. You don't start a vast war-machine functioning in mere hours. We're planning on quick victory with a sudden, devastating atomic attack on the United States."

"I—know."

"I know you know, Georgi. You hardly seem concerned. Even Comrade Zhubin pointed out how nervous you seemed today, and Zhubin usually minds his own business. You seem even worse now."

DORLUP nodded, clearly struggling for words and a way to prolong the conversation, "I—I'm not myself," he said, mopping his brow.

"Well," said Chenkov, irritably, "is that all you wanted me for?"

Dorlup stood there, fidgeting, Chenkov snorted, began to leave the room.

"Just one moment, Comrade Marshal." It was Tedor, who had emerged from behind the drapery.

"Eh? By Lenin, what are you doing here Archevski? Am I going crazy? I thought I sent you to find this, uh—Barwan."

"You did, Comrade Marshal, but—"

"But I told him not to," said Dorlup.

"You? What for? Ruscar wanted him brought at once."

"I know that," said Dorlup.

"But the Comrade Premier told me not to go, anyway. Then Comrade Premier further told me that Ruscar had concluded his usefulness after we had Stalin's resurrected brain. The Comrade Premier—"

"Let him talk for himself, Archevski! And I'll see you later for disobeying my orders."

"No you won't."

"He's in my employ now," Dorlup told Chenkov. "What he was saying is this: why do we need Ruscar? Let Ruscar go back where he came from. We can handle everything ourselves."

"Georgi, you don't mean it."

"I mean it."

"Then you are *not* yourself! You had better see a doctor. Why, only the day before yesterday we spoke with Ruscar about what all this could mean. Defeating the United States. We could conquer the earth, of course. But what is the Earth here and now, this year, when with Ruscar's help we can have all Earth, through all the centuries, for all time?"

"What makes you think we can trust this Ruscar?"

"That's fantastic. Everything is arranged. Perhaps later, much later—after we have consolidated our position in time, then we can think of doing without Ruscar's help. But not now."

"Well—" said Dorlup, at a loss for words.

The door opened. It was Georgi Malenkov who stood there.

"VLADIMIR, I was told I could find you here in con-ference with someone, they didn't know who. They — Vladimir!" Malenkov looked at Dorlup. His small eyes bulged.

Chenkov's mouth dropped open. "This is impossible!"

"Vladimir, please. Please, I see it now, I see it all—" Malenkov had grown pale staring at his duplicate. "You have this double. You and Ruscar. You plan to do away with me and keep a figurehead instead. Vladimir, please, I can listen to reason. I can make my rule a partnership, a triumvirate if you wish." Malenkov was blubbering. "I could smell it in the air, this plot, this intrigue, this—I knew something was afoot. Something I didn't know what. All hands were turned against me, all—"

Tedor ran to the door, closed it, locked it.

"Vladimir, I beg of you—"

"Oh, shut up! I don't know any more about this than you do. You are Malenkov, I know that now. The other man looks like you but doesn't talk like you."

Tedor took Archevski's gun from his own pocket. "You try to figure it out," he said. He gave the gun to Dorlup, who stood watch over Russia's two top leaders.

Tedor ran to the drapes, which hid the dressing alcove, tore them down, ripped them into strips. He bound Chenkov first, hand and foot.

"You realize you haven't a chance, whatever game you're playing," Chenkov said.

Tedor bound Malenkov, then fastened them together, sitting on the floor, back to back. If one of them struggled with his bonds he would strangle the other, for Tedor had tied their necks together.

"Give me the gun, Dorlup," he said, taking the pistol. "I haven't time, I can't play with you. I want you to answer one question and I'm going to give you ten seconds to start talking. If you don't, I'll kill you."

Chenkov squirmed, making Malenkov gasp and choke, Chenkov subsided. "What's your question?"

"I want to know the location of your storage areas for atomic weapons."

"N—never!" Malenkov gasped, his voice breaking.

Tedor started counting. "One, two, three, four, five—"

"Wait!" This was Chenkov. "There's no need making a martyr of yourself, Georgi. You tell me, what good would the information do them? They'll never get a chance to use it."

"Y—yes. Don't move, Vladimir. You're choking me, I see what you mean. Very well, this is the information. We have three atomic storehouses, one in the Urals at—"

The information memorized, Tedor forced a gag of drapery material into Chenkov's mouth and one into Malenkov's. With Dorlup he left the study.

"But why did they give us the information so readily?" the solidio writer demanded.

"That's simple. Evidently, they've already removed their atomic weapons from the storage areas, possibly to airfields. They aren't familiar enough with time travel, though. We'll simply go back a dozen hours and blast those three locations. If Russia doesn't have atomic power for a sneak attack, she won't be able to attack at all. First stop is the Lubianka prison, however."

They found Lubianka Street after getting a vehicle from the Kremlin motor pool, the motor officer's eyes bulged when Malenkov and his personal body guard came down for the car themselves. They rushed inside the prison, where the warden demanded, stuttering:

"Is—is this an inspection, C-comrades? We are r-ready at anytime, of course, and honored, even, but sometimes, once in a while, you see—"

"Forget it," Tedor cut him short. "You have a woman prisoner, Anna Myinkov? Bring her to us, quickly."

"At once."

The warden was gone less than ten minutes, returning with a muscular, sexless female jailer who prodded Laniq ahead of her. Laniq stared at them dully, without hope.

"Thank you," said Tedor to the warden. "We'll take her."

Dorlup-Malenkov smiled and the warden bowed out. In the street, Laniq's spirit had returned. "Don't tell me Malenkov himself is going to be around for the execution?"

They didn't say anything. Tedor wanted to be in the car before they revealed themselves to her.

"You'll have to catch me first!" cried Laniq. Tedor had been holding her loosely by the arm and she suddenly tried to pull away. When his grip tightened, she turned on him furiously, raking his face with her nails, kicking, biting butting with her head.

Tedor pinned her arms to her sides while she cried in rage. "Cut it out, Laniq. I'm Tedor. Tedor!"

"Te-dor? Tedor? Oh, Tedor..." Laniq fainted in his arms.

They drove south with her to the time-conveyor.

CHAPTER SIXTEEN

THEY were twelve hours into the past, materializing abruptly on the field of the first atomic area.

Soldiers rushed the conveyor, but when the door opened and Malenkov stood revealed in the entrance, they saluted smartly. "Bring your commanding officer," said Dorlup, and when the man came—a full Marshal—Dorlup ordered three of the most powerful atomic bombs for the conveyor.

They were brought on flatcars, jerry-rigged to the conveyor's bottom at Tedor's direction, with a crude releasing device.

"This is—is somewhat irregular," said the Marshal.

Dorlup said nothing, looked at him scornfully.

"I am sorry, Comrade Premier."

"You should be."

They closed themselves within the conveyor, set the first of their atomic bombs for ten seconds, retreated thirty seconds into the past and took off.

In forty seconds they had climbed to thirty thousand feet. Intense light engulfed the conveyor as it sped away, followed almost at once by a shock wave which buffeted them helplessly about the cabin of the conveyor. Below them and now far to their left, a great atomic mushroom billowed into the sky, then slowed, rising serenely on a brown and violet pillar.

"Let's hit the next one," said Tedor and they did so.

The third storage area was far out beyond the Ural Mountains and to the North, in the remote Siberian wilderness of the great Eurasian landmass. They retreated back into time far enough to account for the two hours it took them to rocket from the Urals to Siberia, then circled over the storage areas while searchlights probed the sky for them like groping fingers.

"That way," Tedor explained, "all the plants will blow up simultaneously, with no chance for one to warn another."

They circled, and Dorlup said, "I'm bringing her down."

"Just a minute." It was Laniq, sitting near the telio, "Someone's calling." A face flashed into view on the screen—Ruscar.

"Let me speak to Barwan," he said. "You have a few seconds to decide whether you want to live or die."

"Take the conveyor back up." Tedor told Dorlup, and went to the telio, Ruscar looked far from happy.

"Tedor, you still have a chance. I've been following you in time, ever since we found out what happened to Malenkov and Chenkov. You can't stop me now, Tedor. Everything is ready and there are enough atom and hydrogen bombs here at this one base to do the job."

Tedor was looking at Ruscar for the first time since his dual life had been revealed. Enemy of time tyrants on the one hand, tyrant who wanted all the world and all of time under his control in the other.

"Throw in with me, Tedor. I'll forget what you've done. We need men like you."

Tedor shook his head. "It would take me years to tell you what I think of you, so I won't even try. The answer is no."

"My conveyor is five miles to the south, Tedor. We're going to blow you out of the sky unless you—"

Tedor snapped the telio off, went to the controls and replaced Dorlup at them.

"Can he do it?" Laniq wanted to know.

Through the port, they watched the other conveyor streak into view. Suddenly there was a rattling noise and a furious hissing as Ruscar opened up with rockets and machine guns. Cursing, Tedor clutched at the controls and their conveyor plummeted towards the earth.

"We're not armed," Dorlup wailed. "He can destroy us at his leisure."

"Maybe." Tedor brought them down to within a few hundred feet of the ground, Ruscar right behind them. The lack of anti-aircraft fire meant Ruscar had ordered the ground batteries out of action, since they might just as easily have hit him.

Ruscar's craft opened up again. A rocket ripped into the hull of their conveyor and exploded, flipping it in a quick 360 degree turn and flinging Tedor from the controls.

He climbed groggily to hands and knees, dragged himself back to the pilot chair. Laniq was stretched out on the floor, moaning. Dorlup sat dazed in a corner. But by the time

Tedor sat at the instrument panel again, Laniq was on her feet groggily at his side.

"Bad?" She said.

"We're helpless, unless we can out-maneuver him."

They dived again. Tedor brought them out of it at the last moment, plunging them half a minute into the past. Ruscar had stayed with them all the way.

"All I need is time to release the bomb and get away, but he's sticking."

Machine gun bullets ripped in through their hull, unarmed since the conveyor was not intended for aerial battle. Tedor forced the craft into a steep climb, then brought it down again in the same maneuver. But Ruscar fled into the past with him and he could not destroy the storage area and Ruscar's conveyor without also killing himself, Laniq and Dorlup in the process.

Ruscar was fast converting their conveyor into a sieve and Tedor realized it would be only moments before he damaged their engine and forced them to crash. They climbed once more, dove again. Laniq looked at Tedor, tears in her eyes. They had come so close to victory…

Tedor punched the controls rapidly. The conveyor rocked, absorbed another rocket hit, shuddered. Then for an instant, it was floating calmly in undisturbed air.

Tedor released the bomb and sent the ship skyward.

"What did you do?" Laniq cried.

"Ruscar figured I'd leap into the past again, I didn't. I tried the future, because it was our only chance. Just fifty seconds, but by the time Ruscar realizes his mistake, I hope…"

They looked down below them, saw a tiny dot which was Ruscar's ship materialize. Then it was blotted out, along with the storage area, by a flash of light, a roar, a seething, rocking, thundering tempest—

Ruscar's conveyor, the storage area, the barren tundra below them—all were replaced by a huge, mushroom-topped pillar of kaleidoscoping destruction…

MUCH later, in southwestern United States:

"My father is going to be all right, Tedor. And have you seen the headlines?"

"Yes." He smiled at her. "There were three mysterious atomic explosions, almost simultaneous, in the USSR. Malenkov and Chenkov have become extremely conciliatory."

"The people of the world will never know what happened."

"Neither will Ruscar. He'd closed the year 1955, intending to move into it in the normal time-stream, sure it would be the crucial year. He died in 1954."

"Then, everything is fine—except for all those trophies I have, Tedor. We could set up a museum, I suppose."

"What for? Those trophies are more valuable where they came from. I can't think of a better way to spend the first few weeks of our married life than to return them. Sort of a honeymoon in time." And Tedor took her in his arms.

She pulled away from him. "Just a minute, Tedor Barwan! I'm not going to kiss anyone until he removes that disguise."

Tedor smiled at her, turned to Dorlup. "You'd better do the same thing, Comrade Malenkov, unless you want the people around here to lynch you."

"I sure will," Dorlup said. "Wait till you see the solidio I'm going to write, though. We'll call it 1954. What a story!"

"Oh, no," groaned Tedor.

But Laniq kissed him and Tedor forgot everything else…

THE END

A DEADLY INTERPLANETARY PLAGUE!

When the dreaded blue plague was discovered on the planet of Dara, rampant fear struck its planetary neighbors. It was an unreasonable and seemingly uncontrollable fear that soon led to an uncontrollable hatred. A hatred that eventually threatened the lives of millions and endangered the peace of the whole galaxy.

Renown science fiction author Murrary Leinster spins another in his long line of medical sci-fi tales, laced with a generous helping of interplanetary intrigue.

ABOUT MURRAY LEINSTER

Murray Leinster...

...was the pen name of one of the most beloved science fiction and fantasy authors of the 20th Century, William F. Jenkins. As an author, his illustrious career stretched over six imagination-filled decades. Born in 1896, he broke into professional writing just shy of his 20th birthday. Leinster was known primarily for his sci-fi writings, but was also adept in the genres of horror, adventure, and mystery. His career was one of the busiest of the writers of his day and he was known for a consistently high level of storytelling skill. He wrote over 1,500 short stories and articles, 14 movie scripts, and hundreds of radio scripts and teleplays. Leinster was honored with a Hugo Award in 1956 for his memorable novelette, "Exploration Team." In 1995 the Sidewise Award for Alternate History took its name from one of Leinster's classic sci-fi tales, "Sidewise in Time." Murray Leinster passed away in 1975, just shy of his 79th birthday.

PARIAH
PLANET

By
MURRAY LEINSTER

ARMCHAIR FICTION
PO Box 4369, Medford, Oregon 97501-0168

*For more information about Armchair Books and products, visit our
website at…*

www.armchairfiction.com

Or email us at…

armchairfiction@yahoo.com

CHAPTER ONE

The little Med Ship came out of overdrive and the stars were strange and the Milky Way seemed unfamiliar. Which, of course, was because the Milky Way and the local Cepheid marker-stars were seen from an unaccustomed angle and a not-yet-commonplace pattern of varying magnitudes. But Calhoun grunted in satisfaction. There was a banded sun off to port, which was good. A breakout at no more than sixty light-hours from one's destination wasn't bad, in a strange sector of the Galaxy and after three light-years of journeying blind.

"Arise and shine, Murgatroyd," said Calhoun. "Comb your whiskers. Get set to astonish the natives!"

A sleepy, small, shrill voice said;

"*Chee!*"

Murgatroyd the *tormal* came crawling out of his small cubbyhole. He blinked at Calhoun.

"We're due to land shortly," Calhoun observed. "You'll impress the local inhabitants. I'll be unpopular. According to the records, there's been no Med Ship inspection here for twelve standard years. And that was practically no inspection, to judge by the report."

Murgatroyd said;

"*Chee-chee!*"

He began to make his toilet, first licking his right-hand whiskers and then his left. Then he stood up and shook himself and looked interestedly at Calhoun. *Tormals* are companionable small animals. They are charmed when somebody speaks to them. They find great, deep satisfaction in imitating the actions of humans, as parrots and mynahs and parrokets imitate human speech. But *tormals* have certain useful, genetically transmitted talents which make them much more valuable than mere companions or pets.

Calhoun got a light-reading for the banded sun. It could hardly be an accurate measure of distance, but it was a guide. He said;

"Hold on to something, Murgatroyd!"

Calhoun threw the overdrive switch and the Med Ship flicked back into that questionable state of being in which velocities of some hundreds of times that of light are possible. The sensation of going into overdrive was unpleasant. A moment later, the sensation of coming out was no less so. Calhoun had experienced it often enough, and still didn't like it.

The sun Weald burned huge and terrible in space. It was close, now. Its disk covered half a degree of arc.

"Very neat," observed Calhoun. "Weald Three is our port, Murgatroyd. The plane of the ecliptic would be— Hm..."

He swung the outside electron telescope, picked up a nearby bright object, enlarged its image to show details, and checked it against the local star-pilot. He calculated a moment. The distance was too short for even the briefest of overdrive hops, but it would take time to get there on solar-system drive.

He thumbed down the communicator-button and spoke into a microphone.

"Med Ship Aesclipus Twenty reporting arrival and asking coördinates for landing. Purpose of landing, planetary health inspection. Our mass is fifty tons standard. We should arrive at a landing position in something under four hours. Repeat. Med Ship Aesclipus Twenty..."

He finished the regular second transmission and made coffee for himself while he waited for an answer. Murgatroyd wanted a cup of coffee too. Murgatroyd adored coffee. He held a tiny cup in a furry small paw and sipped gingerly at the hot liquid.

A voice came out of the communicator;

"*Aesclipus Twenty, repeat your identification!*"

Calhoun went to the control-board.

"Aesclipus Twenty," he said patiently, "is a Med Ship, sent by the Interstellar Medical Service to make a planetary health inspection on Weald. Check with your public health authorities. This is the first Med Ship visit in twelve standard years, I believe, which is inexcusable. But your health authorities will know all about it. Check with them."

The voice said truculently;

"*What was your last port?*"

Calhoun named it. This was not his home sector, but Sector Twelve had gotten into a very bad situation. Some of its planets had gone unvisited for as long as twenty years, and twelve between inspections was almost common-place. Other sectors had been called on to help it catch up. Calhoun was one of the loaned Med Ship men, and because of the emergency he'd been given a list of half a dozen planets to be inspected one after another, instead of reporting back to sector headquarters after each visit. He'd had minor troubles before with landing-grid operators in Sector Twelve.

So he was very patient. He named the planet last inspected, the one from which he'd set out for Weald Three. The voice from the communicator said sharply;

"*What port before that?*"

Calhoun named the one before the last.

"*Don't drive any closer,*" said the voice harshly, "*or you'll be destroyed!*"

Calhoun said coldly;

"Now you listen to me, friend! I'm from the Interstellar Medical Service! You get in touch with planetary health services immediately! Remind them of the Interstellar

Medical Inspection Agreement, signed on Tralee two hundred and forty standard years ago. Remind them that if they do not cooperate in medical inspection that I can put your planet under quarantine and your space commerce will be cut off like that! No ship will be cleared for Weald from any other planet in the galaxy until there has been a health inspection! Things have pretty well gone to pot so far as the Med Service in this sector is concerned, but we're trying to straighten it out. You have twenty minutes to clear this and then, I'm coming in. If I'm not landed, a quarantine goes on! Tell your health authorities that!"

Silence. Calhoun clicked off and poured himself another cup of coffee. Murgatroyd held out his cup for a refill. Calhoun gave it to him.

"I hate to put on an official hat, Murgatroyd," he said annoyedly, "but there are some people who won't have any other way."

Murgatroyd said "*Chee!*" and sipped at his cup.

Calhoun checked the course of the Med Ship. It bored on through space. There were tiny noises from the communicator. There were whisperings and rustlings and the occasional strange and sometimes beautiful musical notes whose origin is yet obscure, but which, since they are carried by electromagnetic radiation of wildly varying wave-lengths, are not likely to be the fabled music of the spheres. He waited.

In fifteen minutes a different voice came from the speaker. "*Med Ship Aesclipus! Med Ship Aesclipus!*"

Calhoun answered and the voice said anxiously;

"'*Sorry about the challenge, but we have the blueskin problem always with us. We have to be extremely careful! Will you come in, please?*"

"I'm on my way," said Calhoun.

"*The planetary health authorities,*" said the voice, more anxiously still, "*are very anxious to be coöperative. We need Med*

Service help! We lose a lot of sleep over the blueskins! Could you tell us the name of the last Med Ship to land here, and its inspector, and when that inspection was made? We want to look up the record of the event to be able to assist you in every possible way."

"He's lying," Calhoun told Murgatroyd, "but he's more scared than hostile."

He picked up the order-folio on Weald Three. He gave the information about the last Med Ship visit. He clicked off.

"What?" he asked, "is a blueskin?"

He'd read the folio on Weald, of course, but as the ship swam onward through emptiness he went through it again. The last medical inspection had been only perfunctory. Twelve years earlier—instead of three—a Med Ship had landed on Weald. There had been official conferences with health officials. There was a report on the birth-rate, the death-rate, the anomaly-rate, and a breakdown of all reported communicable diseases. But that was all. There were no special comments and no overall picture.

Presently Calhoun found the word in a Sector dictionary, where words of only local usage were to be found.

"Blueskin; Colloquial term for a person recovered from a plague which left large patches of blue pigment irregularly distributed over the body. Especially, inhabitants of Dara. The condition is said to be caused by a chronic, non-fatal form of Dara plague and has been said to be non-infectious, though this is not certain. The etiology of Dara plague has not fully been worked out. The blueskin condition is hereditary but not a genetic modification, as markings appear in non-Mendellian distributions..."

Calhoun puzzled over it. Nobody could have read the entire Sector directory, even with unlimited leisure during travel between solar systems. Calhoun hadn't tried. But now he went laboriously through indices and cross-references while the ship continued travel onward. He found no other reference to blueskins. He looked up Dara. It was listed as an inhabited planet, some four hundred years colonized, with a landing-grid and at the time the main notice was written out, a flourishing interstellar commerce. But there was a memo, evidently added to the entry in some change of editions.

"Since plague, special license from Med Service is required for landing."

That was all. Absolutely all.

The communicator said suavely;

"*Med Ship Aesclipus Twenty! Come in on vision, please!*"

Calhoun went to the control-board and threw on vision.

"Well, what now?" he demanded.

His screen lighted. A bland face looked out at him.

"*We have—ah—verified your statements,*" said the third voice from Weald. "*Just one more item. Are you alone in your ship?*"

"Of course," said Calhoun, frowning.

"*Quite alone?*" insisted the voice.

"Obviously!" said Calhoun.

"*No other living creature?*" insisted the voice again.

"Of—Oh!" said Calhoun annoyedly. He called over his shoulder. "Murgatroyd! Come here!"

Murgatroyd hopped to his lap and gazed interestedly at the screen. The bland face changed remarkably. The voice changed even more.

"*Very good!*" it said. "*Very, very good! Blueskins do not have tormals! You are Med Service! By all means come in. Your coördinates will be…*"

Calhoun wrote them down. He clicked off the communicator again and growled to Murgatroyd;

"So I might have been a blueskin, eh? And you're my passport, because only Med Ships have members of your tribe aboard! What the hell's the matter, Murgatroyd? They act like they think somebody's trying to get down on their planet with a load of plague-germs!"

He grumbled to himself for minutes. The life of a Med Ship man is not exactly a sinecure, at best. It means long periods in empty space in overdrive, which is absolute and deadly tedium. Then two or three days aground, checking official documents and statistics, and asking questions to see how many of the newest medical techniques have reached this planet or that, and the supplying of information about such as have not arrived. Then lifting out to space for long periods of tedium, to repeat the process somewhere else. Med Ships carry only one man because two could not stand the close contact without quarreling with each other. But Med Ships do carry *tormals*, like Murgatroyd, and a *tormal* and a man can get along indefinitely, like a man and a dog. It is a highly unequal friendship, but it seems to be satisfactory to both.

Calhoun was very much annoyed with the way the Med Service had been operated in Sector Twelve. He was one of many men at work to correct the results of incompetence in directing Med Service in the twelfth sector. But it is always disheartening to have to labor at making up for somebody else's blundering, when there is so much new work that needs to be done.

The condition shown by the landing-grid suspicions was a case in point. Blueskins were people who inherited a splotchy skin-pigmentation from other people who'd survived a plague. Weald plainly maintained a one-planet quarantine against them. But a quarantine is normally an emergency measure. The Med Service should have taken over, wiped out the need for a quarantine, and then lifted it. It hadn't been done.

Calhoun fumed to himself.

The world of Weald Three grew brighter and brighter and became a disk. The disk had ice-caps and a reasonable proportion of land and water surface. The Med Ship decelerated, and voices notified observation from the surface, and the little craft came to a stop some five planetary diameters out from solidity. The landing-field force-field locked on to it, and its descent began.

The business of landing was all very familiar, from the blue rim which appeared at the limb of the planet from one diameter out, to the singular flowing-apart of the surface features as the ship sank still lower. There was the circular landing-grid, rearing skyward for nearly a mile. It could let down interstellar liners from emptiness and lift them out to emptiness again, with great convenience and economy for everyone.

It landed the Med Ship in its center, and there were officials to greet Calhoun, and he knew in advance the routine part of his visit. There would be an interview with the planet's chief executive, by whatever title he was called. There would be a banquet. Murgatroyd would be petted by everybody. There would be painful efforts to impress Calhoun with the splendid conduct of public health matters on Weald. He would be told much scandal. He might find one man, somewhere, who passionately labored to advance the welfare of his fellow humans by finding out how to keep them well, or failing that how to make them well when they got sick. And in two days, or three, Calhoun would be escorted back to the landing-grid, and lifted out to space, and he'd spend long empty days in overdrive and land somewhere else to do the whole thing all over again.

It all happened exactly as he expected, with one exception. Every human being he met on Weald wanted to talk about blueskins. Blueskins and the idea of blueskins obsessed everyone. Calhoun listened without asking questions until he had the picture of what blueskins meant to the people who talked of them. Then he knew there would be no use asking questions at random. Nobody mentioned ever having seen a blueskin. Nobody mentioned a specific event in which a blueskin had at any named time taken part. But everybody was afraid of blueskins. It was a patterned, an inculcated, a stage-directed fixed idea. And it found expression in shocked references to the vileness, the depravity, the monstrousness of the blueskin inhabitants of Dara, from whom Weald must at all costs be protected.

It did not make sense. So Calhoun listened politely until he found an undistinguished medical man who wanted some special information about gene-selection as practised halfway across the galaxy. He invited that man to the Med Ship, where he supplied the information not hitherto available. He saw his guest's eyes shine a little with that joyous awe a man feels when he finds out something he has wanted long and badly to know.

"Now," said Calhoun, "tell me something! Why does everybody on this planet hate the inhabitants of Dara? It's light-years away. Nobody claims to have suffered in person from them. Why make a point of hating them?"

The Wealdian doctor grimaced.

"They've blue patches on their skins. They're different from us. So they can be pictured as a danger and our political parties can make an election issue out of competing for the privilege of defending us from them. They had a plague on Dara, once. They're accused of still having it ready for export."

"Hm," said Calhoun. "The story is that they want to spread contagion here, eh? Doesn't anybody"—his tone was sardonic—"doesn't anybody urge that they be massacred as an act of piety?"

"Yes—s—s—s," admitted the doctor reluctantly. "It's mentioned in political speeches."

"But how's it rationalized?" demanded Calhoun. "What's the argument to make pigment-patches involve moral and physical degradation, as I'm assured is the case?"

"In the public schools," said the doctor, "the children are taught that blueskins are now carriers of the disease they survived three generations ago! That they hate everybody who isn't a blueskin. That they are constantly scheming to introduce their plague here so most of us will die and the rest become blueskins. That's beyond rationalizing. It can't be true, but it's not safe to doubt it."

"Bad business," said Calhoun coldly. "That sort of thing usually costs lives, in the end. It could lead to massacre!"

"Perhaps it has, in a way," said the doctor unhappily. "One doesn't like to think about it." He paused, and said; "Twenty years ago there was a famine on Dara. There were crop-failures. The situation must have been very bad. They built a space-ship. They've no use for such things normally, because no nearby planet will deal with them or let them land. But they built a space-ship and came here. They went in orbit around Weald. They asked to trade for shiploads of food. They offered any price in heavy metals, gold, platinum, iridium, and so on. They talked from orbit by vision communicators. They could be seen to be blueskins. You can guess what happened!"

"Tell me," said Calhoun.

"We armed ships in a hurry," admitted the doctor, "We chased their space-ship back to Dara. We hung in space off the planet. We told them we'd blast their world from pole to pole if they ever dared take to space again. We made them destroy their one ship, and we watched on visionscreens as it was done."

"But you gave them food?"

"No," said the doctor ashamedly. "They were blueskins."

"How bad was the famine?"

"Who knows? Any number may have starved! And we kept a squadron of armed ships in their skies for years. To keep them from spreading the plague, we said. And some of us believed it, probably!"

The doctor's tone was purest irony.

"Lately," he said, "there's been a move for economy in our government. Simultaneously, we began to have a series of over-abundant crops. The government had to buy the excess grain to keep the price up. Retired patrol-ships—built to watch over Dara—were available for storage-space. We filled them up with grain and sent them out into orbit. They're there now, hundreds of thousands or millions of tons of grain!"

"And Dara?"

The Doctor shrugged. He stood up.

"Our hatred of Dara," he said, again ironically, "has produced one thing. Roughly halfway between here and Dara there's a two-planet solar system, Orede. There's a usable planet there. It was proposed to build an outpost of Weald there, against blueskins. Cattle were landed to run wild and multiply and make a reason for colonists to settle there. They did, but nobody wants to move nearer to blueskins! So Orede stayed uninhabited until a hunting-party shooting wild cattle found an outcropping of heavy-metal ore. So now there's a mine there. And that's all. A few hundred men work the mine at fabulous wages. You may be asked to check on their health. But not Dara's!"

"I see," said Calhoun, frowning.

The doctor moved toward the Med Ship's exit-port.

"I answered your questions," he said grimly. "But if I talked to anyone else as I've done to you, I'd be lucky only to be driven into exile!"

"I shan't give you away," said Calhoun. He did not smile.

When the doctor had gone, Calhoun said deliberately;

"Murgatroyd, you should be grateful that you're a *tormal* and not a man. There's nothing about being a *tormal* to make you ashamed!"

Then he grimly changed his garments for the full-dress uniform of the Med Service. There was to be a banquet at which he would sit next to the planet's chief executive and hear innumerable speeches about the splendor of Weald. Calhoun had his own, strictly Med Service opinion of the planet's latest and most boasted-of achievement. It was a domed city in the polar regions, where nobody ever had to go outdoors. He was less than professionally enthusiastic about the moving streets, and much less approving of the dream-broadcasts which supplied hypnotic, sleep-inducing rhythms to anybody who chose to listen to them. The price was that while asleep one would hear high praise of commercial products, and one might believe them when awake.

But it was not Calhoun's function to criticize when it could be avoided. Med Service had been badly managed in Sector Twelve. So at the banquet Calhoun made a brief and diplomatic address in which he temperately praised what could be praised, and did not mention anything else.

The chief executive followed him. As head of the government he paid some tribute to the Med Service. But then he reminded his hearers proudly of the high culture, splendid health, and remarkable prosperity of the planet since his political party took office. This, he said, was in spite of the need to be perpetually on guard against the greatest and most immediate danger to which any world in all the galaxy was exposed. He referred to the blueskins, of course. He did not need to tell the people of Weald what vigilance, what constant watchfulness was necessary against that race of depraved and malevolent deviants from the norm of humanity. But Weald, he said with emotion, held aloft the torch of all that humanity held most dear, and defended not alone the lives of its people against blueskin contagion, but their noble heritage of ideals against Blueskin pollution.

When he sat down, Calhoun said very politely;

"It looks like some day it should be practical politics to urge the massacre of all blueskins. Have you thought of that?"

The chief executive said comfortably;

"The idea's been proposed. It's good politics to urge it, but it would be foolish to carry it out. People vote against blueskins. Wipe them out, and where'd you be?"

Calhoun ground his teeth, quietly.

There were more speeches. Then a messenger, white-faced, arrived with a written note for the chief executive. He read it and passed it to Calhoun. It was from the Ministry of Health. The space-port reported that a ship had just broken out from overdrive within the Wealdian solar system. Its tape-transmitter had automatically signalled its arrival from the mining-planet Orede. But, having sent off its automatic signal, the ship lay dead in space. It did not drive toward Weald. It did not respond to signals. It drifted like a derelict upon no course at all. It seemed ominous, and since it came from Orede—the planet nearest to Dara of the blueskins—the health ministry informed the planet's chief executive.

"It'll be blueskins," said that astute person, firmly. "They're next-door to Orede. That's who's done this. It wouldn't surprise me if they'd seeded Orede with their plague, and this ship came from there to give us warning!"

"There's no evidence for anything of the sort," protested Calhoun. "A ship simply came out of overdrive and didn't signal further. That's all."

"We'll see," said the chief executive ominously. "We'll go directly to the spaceport."

Calhoun retrieved Murgatroyd who had been visiting with the wives of the higher-up officials. His small paunch distended with cakes and coffee and such delicacies as he'd been plied with. He was half comatose from over-feeding and over-petting, but he was glad to see Calhoun. At the spaceport they discovered the situation remained unchanged.

A ship from Orede had come out of overdrive and lay dead in emptiness. It did not answer calls. It did not move in space. It floated eerily in no orbit around anything, going nowhere; doing nothing. And panic was the consequence.

It seemed to Calhoun that the official handling of the matter accounted for the terror that he could feel building up. The so-far-unexplained bit of news was on the air all over the planet Weald. There was nobody awake of all the world's population who did not believe that there was a new danger in the sky. Nobody doubted that it came from blueskins. The treatment of the news was precisely calculated to keep alive the hatred of Weald for the inhabitants of the world Dara.

Calhoun put Murgatroyd into the Med Ship and went back to the spaceport office. A small space-boat, designed to inspect the circling grain-ships from time, was already aloft. The landing-grid had thrust it swiftly out most of the way. Now it droned and drove on sturdily toward the enigmatic ship.

Calhoun took no part in the agitated conferences among the officials and news reporters at the space-port. But he listened to the talk about him. As the investigating small ship drew nearer and nearer to the deathly-still cargo vessel, the guesses about the meaning of its breakout and following silence grew more and more wild. But, singularly, there was not one suggestion that the mystery might not be the work of blueskins. Blueskins were scapegoats for all the fears and all the uneasiness a perhaps over-civilized world developed.

Presently the investigating space-boat reached the mystery ship and circled it, beaming queries. No answer. It reported the cargo-ship dark. No lights shone anywhere on or in it. There were no induction-surges from even pulsing, idling engines. Delicately, the messenger-craft maneuvered until it touched the silent vessel. It reported that microphones detected no motion whatever inside.

"Let a volunteer go aboard," commanded the chief executive. "Have him report what he finds."

A pause. Then the solemn announcement of an intrepid volunteer's name, from far, far away. Calhoun listened, frowning darkly. This pompous heroism wouldn't be noticed in the Med Service. It would be routine behavior.

Suspenseful, second-by-second reports. The volunteer had rocketed himself across the emptiness between the two again-separated ships. He had opened the airlock from outside. He'd gone in. He'd closed the outer airlock door. He'd opened the inner. He reported.

The relayed report was almost incoherent, what with horror and incredulity and the feeling of doom that came upon the volunteer. The ship was a bulk-cargo ore-carrier, designed to run between Orede and Weald with cargoes of heavy-metal ores and a crew of no more than five men. There was no cargo in her holds now, though. Instead, there were men. They packed the ship. They filled the corridors. They had crawled into every cargo and other space where a man could find room to push himself. There were hundreds of them. It was insanity. And it had been greater insanity still for the ship to have taken off with so preposterous a load of living creatures.

But they weren't living any longer. The air apparatus had been designed for a crew of five. It could purify the air for possibly twenty or more. But there were hundreds of men in hiding as well as in plain view in the cargo-ship from Orede.

There were many, many times more than her air apparatus and reserve tanks could possibly have serviced. They couldn't even have been fed during the journey from Orede to Weald!

But they hadn't starved. Air-scarcity killed them before the ship came out of overdrive.

A remarkable thing was that there was no written message in the ship's log which referred to its take-off. There was no memorandum of the taking on of such an impossible number of passengers.

"The blueskins did it," said the chief executive of Weald. He was pale. All about Calhoun men looked sick and shocked and terrified. "It was the blueskins! We'll have to teach them a lesson!" Then he turned to Calhoun. "The volunteer who went on that ship... He'll have to stay there, won't he? He can't be brought back to Weald without bringing contagion..."

Calhoun raged at him.

CHAPTER TWO

There was a certain coldness in the manner of those at the Weald spaceport when the Med Ship left next morning. Calhoun was not popular because Weald was scared. It had been conditioned to scare easily, where blueskins might be involved. Its children were trained to react explosively when the word "blueskin" was uttered in their hearing, and its adults tended to say "blueskin" when anything cause uneasiness entered their minds. So a planet-wide habit of non-rational response had formed and was not seen to be irrational because almost everybody had it.

The volunteer who'd discovered the tragedy on the ship from Orede was safe, though. He'd made a completely conscientious survey of the ship he'd volunteered to enter and examine. For his courage, he'd have been doomed but for Calhoun. The reaction of his fellow-citizens was that by entering the ship he might have become contaminated by blueskin infective material if the plague still existed, and if the men in the ship had caught it—but they certainly hadn't died of it—and if there had been blueskins on Orede to communicate it—for which there was no evidence—and if blueskins were responsible for the tragedy. Which was at the moment pure supposition. But Weald feared he might bring death back to Weald if he were allowed to return.

Calhoun saved his life. He ordered that the guard-ship admit him to its airlock, which then was to be filled with steam and chlorine. The combination would sterilize and partly even eat away his space-suit, after which the chlorine and steam should be bled out to space, and air from the ship let into the lock. If he stripped off the space-suit without touching its outer surface, and reëntered the investigating ship while the suit was flung outside by a man in another space-suit, handling it with a pole he'd fling after it, there could be no possible contamination brought back.

Calhoun was quite right, but Weald in general considered that he'd persuaded the government to take an unreasonable risk.

There were other reasons for disapproving of him. Calhoun had been unpleasantly frank. The coming of the death-ship stirred to frenzy those people who believed that all blueskins should be exterminated as a pious act. They'd appeared on every visionscreen, citing not only the ship from Orede but other incidents which they interpreted as crimes against Weald. They demanded that all Wealdian atomic reactors be modified to turn out fusion-bomb materials while a space-fleet was made ready for an anti-blueskin crusade. They confidently demanded such a rain of fusion-bombs on Dara that no blueskin, no animal, no shred of vegetation, no fish in the deepest ocean, not even a living virus-particle of the blueskin plague could remain alive on the blueskin world!

One of these vehement orators even asserted that Calhoun agreed that no other course was possible, speaking for the Interstellar Medical Service. And Calhoun furiously demanded a chance to deny it by broadcast, and he made a bitter and indiscreet speech from which a planet-wide audience inferred that he thought them fools. He did.

So he was definitely unpopular when his ship lifted from Weald. He'd curtly given his destination as Orede, from which the death-ship had come. The landing-grid locked on, raised the small space-craft until Weald was a great shining ball below it, and then somehow scornfully cast him off. The Med Ship was free, in clear space where there was not enough of a gravitational field to hinder overdrive.

He aimed for his destination, his face very grim. He said savagely;

"Get set, Murgatroyd! Overdrive coming!"

He thumbed down the overdrive button. The universe of stars went out, while everything living in the ship felt the customary sensations of dizziness, of nausea, and of a spiralling fall to nothingness. Then there was silence. The Med Ship actually moved at a rate which was a preposterous number of times the speed of light, but it felt absolutely solid, absolutely firm and fixed. A ship in overdrive feels exactly as if it were buried deep in the core of a planet. There is no vibration. There is no sign of anything but solidity and—if one looks out a port—there is only utter blackness plus an absence of sound fit to make one's eardrums crack.

But within seconds random tiny noises began. There was a reel and there were sound-speakers to keep the ship from sounding like a grave. The reel played and the speakers gave off minute creakings, and meaningless hums, and very tiny noises of every imaginable sort, all of which were just above the threshold of the inaudible.

Calhoun fretted. Sector Twelve was in very bad shape. A conscientious Med Service man would never have let the anti-blueskin obsession go unmentioned in a report on Weald. Health is not only a physical affair. There is mental health, also. When mental health goes a civilization can be destroyed more surely and more terribly than by any imaginable war or plague-germ. A plague kills off those who are susceptible to it, leaving immunes to build up a world again. But immunes are the first to be killed when a mass neurosis sweeps a population.

Weald was definitely a Med Service problem world. Dara was another. And when hundreds of men jammed themselves into a cargo-boat which could not furnish them with air to breathe, and took off and went into overdrive before the air could fail... Orede called for no less of worry.

"I think," said Calhoun dourly, "that I'll have some coffee."

"Coffee" was one of the words that Murgatroyd recognized immediately. He would usually watch the coffee-maker with bright, interested eyes. He'd even tried to imitate Calhoun's motions with it, once, and had scorched his paws in the attempt. This time he did not move.

Calhoun turned his head. Murgatroyd sat on the floor, his long tail coiled reflectively about a chair-leg. He watched the door of the Med Ship's sleeping-cabin.

"Murgatroyd," said Calhoun. "I mentioned coffee!"

"*Chee!*" shrilled Murgatroyd.

But he continued to look at the door. The temperature was kept lower in the other cabin, and the look of things was different from the control-compartment. The difference was part of the means by which a man was able to be alone for weeks on end—alone save for his *tormal*—without becoming ship-happy. There were other carefully thought out items in the ship with the same purpose. But none of them should cause Murgatroyd to stare fixedly and fascinatedly at the sleeping-cabin door. Not when coffee was in the making!

Calhoun considered. He became angry at the immediate suspicion that occurred to him. As a Med Service man, he was duty-bound to be impartial. To be impartial might mean not to side absolutely with Weald in its enmity to blueskins. The people of Weald had refused to help Dara in a time of famine; they'd blockaded that pariah world for years afterward; they had other reasons for hating the people they'd treated badly. It was entirely reasonable for some fanatic on Weald to consider that Calhoun must be killed lest he be of help to the blueskins Weald abhorred.

In fact, it was quite possible that somebody had stowed away on the Med Ship to murder Calhoun, so that there would be no danger of any report favorable to Dara ever being presented anywhere. If so, such a stowaway would be in the sleeping-cabin now, waiting for Calhoun to walk unsuspiciously in to be shot dead.

So Calhoun made coffee. He slipped a blaster into a pocket where it would be handy. He filled a small cup for Murgatroyd and a large one for himself, and then a second large one.

He tapped on the sleeping-cabin door, standing aside lest a blaster-bolt came through it.

"Coffee's ready," he said sardonically. "Come out and join us."

There was a long pause. Calhoun rapped again.

"You've a seat at the captain's table," he said more sardonically still. "It's not polite to keep me waiting!"

He listened, alert for a rush which would be a fanatic's desperate attempt to do murder despite premature discovery. He was prepared to shoot quite ruthlessly.

But there was no rush. Instead, there came hesitant foot-falls. The door of the cabin slid slowly aside. A girl appeared in the opening, desperately white and desperately composed.

"H-how did you know I was there?" she asked shakily. She moistened her lips. "You didn't see me! I was in a closet, and you didn't even enter the room!"

Calhoun said grimly;

"I've sources of information." He pointed to Murgatroyd.

The girl did not move. Her eyes went from Murgatroyd to Calhoun.

"And now," said Calhoun, "do you want to tell me your story? You have one ready, I'm sure."

"There—there isn't any," said the girl unsteadily. "Just—I—I need to get to Orede, and you're going there. There's no other way to go—now."

"To the contrary," said Calhoun, "there'll undoubtedly be a fleet heading for Orede as soon as it can be assembled and armed. But I'm afraid that's not a very good story. Try another."

She shivered a little.

"I'm—running away…"

"Ah!" said Calhoun. "In that case I'll take you back."

"No!" she said fiercely. "I'll—I'll die first! I'll wreck this ship first!"

Her hand came from behind her. There was a tiny blaster in it. But it shook visibly as she tried to aim it.

"I'll—shoot out the controls!"

Calhoun blinked. He'd had to make a drastic change in his estimate of the situation the instant he saw that the stowaway was a girl. Now he had to make another when her threat was not to kill him but to disable the ship. Women are rarely assassins, and when they are they don't use energy weapons. Daggers and poisons are more typical.

"I'd rather you didn't do that," said Calhoun drily. "Besides, you'd get deadly bored if we were stuck in a derelict waiting for our air and food to give out."

Murgatroyd, for no reason whatever, felt it necessary to enter the conversation. He said;

"*Chee-chee-chee!*"

"A very sensible suggestion," observed Calhoun. "We'll sit down and have a cup of coffee." To the girl he said, "I'll take you to Orede, since that's where you say you want to go."

"I—there's a boy there—"

Calhoun shook his head.

"No," he said reprovingly. "Nearly all the mining colony had packed itself into the ship that came into Weald with everybody dead. But not all. And there's been no check of what men were in the ship and what men weren't. You wouldn't go to Orede if it were likely your fellow had died on the way to you. Here's your coffee. Sugar or saccho, and do you take cream?"

She trembled a little, but she took the cup.

"I—don't understand—"

"Murgatroyd and I," explained Calhoun—and he did not know whether he spoke out of anger or something else—"we are do-gooders. We go around trying to keep people from getting killed. It's our profession. We practise it even on our own behalf. We want to stay alive. So since you make such drastic threats, we will take you where you want to go. Especially since we're going there anyhow."

"You—don't believe anything I've said!" It was a statement.

"Not a word," admitted Calhoun. "But you'll probably tell us something more believable presently. When did you eat last?"

"Yesterday—"

"Better have something now. We'll talk more later." Calhoun showed her how to punch the readier for such-and-such dishes, to be extracted from storage and warmed or chilled, as the case might be, and served at dialed-for intervals.

Calhoun deliberately immersed himself in the Galactic Directory, looking up the planet Orede. He was headed there, but he'd had no reason to inform himself about it before. Now he read with every appearance of absorption.

The girl ate daintily. Murgatroyd watched with highly amiable interest. But she looked acutely uncomfortable.

Calhoun finished with the Directory. He got out the microfilm reels which contained more information. He was specifically after the Med Service history of all the planets in this sector. He went through the filmed record of every inspection ever made on Weald and on Dara. But Sector Twelve had not been well-run. There was no adequate account of a plague which had wiped out three-quarters of the population of an inhabited planet! It had happened shortly after one Med Ship visit, and was over before another Med Ship came by. But there should have been painstaking investigation, even after the fact. There should have been a collection of infective material and a reasonably complete identification and study of the infective agent. It hadn't been made. There was probably some other emergency at the time, and it slipped by. But Calhoun—whose career was not to be spent in this sector—resolved on a blistering report about this negligence and its consequences.

He kept himself casually busy, ignoring the girl. A Med Ship man has resources of study and meditation with which to occupy himself during overdrive travel from one planet to another. Calhoun made use of those resources. He acted as if he were completely unconscious of the stowaway. But Murgatroyd watched her with charmed attention.

Hours after her discovery, she said uneasily;

"Please?"

Calhoun looked up.

"Yes?"

"I—don't know exactly how things stand."

"You are a stowaway," said Calhoun. "Legally, I have the right to put you out the airlock. It doesn't seem necessary. There's a cabin. When you're sleepy, use it. Murgatroyd and I can make out quite well here. When you're hungry, you now know how to get something to eat. When we land on Orede, you'll probably go about whatever business you have there. That's all."

She stared at him.

"But—you don't believe what I've told you!"

"No," agreed Calhoun. But he didn't add to the statement.

"But—I will tell you," she offered. "The police were after me. I had to get away from Weald! I had to! I'd stolen—"

He shook his head.

"No," he said. "If you were a thief, you'd say anything in the world except that you were a thief. You're not ready to tell the truth yet. You don't have to, so why tell me anything? I suggest that you get some sleep."

She rose slowly. Twice her lips parted as if to speak again, but then she went into the other cabin and closed herself in.

Murgatroyd blinked at the place where she'd disappeared and then climbed up into Calhoun's lap, with complete assurance of welcome. He settled himself and was silent for moments. Then he said;

"*Chee!*"

"I believe you're right," said Calhoun. "She doesn't belong on Weald, or with the conditioning she'd have had, there'd be only one place she'd dread worse than Orede, and that would be Dara. But I doubt she'd be afraid to land even on Dara."

Murgatroyd liked to be talked to. He liked to pretend that he carried on a conversation, like humans.

"*Chee-chee!*" he said with conviction.

"Definitely," agreed Calhoun. "She's not doing this for her personal advantage. Whatever she thinks she's doing, it's more important to her than her own life. Murgatroyd—"

"*Chee?*" said Murgatroyd in an inquiring tone.

"There are wild cattle on Orede," said Calhoun. "Herds and herds of them. I have a suspicion that somebody's been shooting them. Lots of them. Do you agree? Don't you think that a lot of cattle have been slaughtered on Orede lately?"

Murgatroyd yawned. He settled himself still more comfortably in Calhoun's lap.

"*Chee,*" he said drowsily.

He went to sleep, while Calhoun continued the examination of highly condensed information. Presently he looked up the normal rate of increase, with other data, among herds of *bivis domesticus* in a wild state, on planets where they have no natural enemies. It wasn't unheard-of for a world to be stocked with useful types of Terran fauna and flora before it was attempted to be colonized. Terran life-forms could play the devil with alien ecological systems, very much to humanity's benefit. Familiar microörganisms and a standard vegetation added to the practicality of human settlements on otherwise alien worlds. But sometimes the results were strange.

They weren't often so strange, however, as to cause some hundreds of men to pack themselves frantically aboard a cargo-ship which couldn't possibly sustain them, so that every man must die while the ship was in overdrive.

Still, by the time Calhoun turned in on a spare pneumatic mattress, he had calculated that as few as a dozen head of cattle, turned loose on a suitable planet, would have increased to herds of thousands or tens or even hundreds of thousands in much less time than had probably elapsed.

The Med Ship drove on in seemingly absolute solidity, with no sound from without, with no sight to be seen outside, with no evidence at all that it was not buried deep in the heart of a planet instead of flashing through emptiness at a speed so great as to have no meaning.

Next ship-day the girl looked oddly at Calhoun when she appeared in the control-room. "Shall I—have breakfast?" she asked uncertainly.

"Why not?"

Silently, she operated the food-readier. She ate. Calhoun gave the impression that he would respond politely when spoken to, but that he was busy with activities that kept him remote from stowaways.

About noon, ship-time, she asked;

"When will we get to Orede?"

Calhoun told her absently, as if he were thinking of something else.

"What—what do you think happened there? I mean, to make that tragedy in the ship?"

"I don't know," said Calhoun. "But I disagree with the authorities on Weald. I don't think it was a planned atrocity of the blueskins."

"Wh-what are blueskins?"

Calhoun turned around and looked at her directly.

"When lying," he said mildly, "you tell as much by what you pretend isn't, as by what you pretend is. You know what blueskins are!"

"B—but what do you think they are?" she asked.

"There used to be a human disease called smallpox," said Calhoun. "When people recovered from it, they were usually marked. Their skin had little scar-pits here and there. At one time, back on Earth, it was expected that everybody would catch smallpox sooner or later, and a large percentage would die of it. And it was so much a matter of course that if they printed a description of a criminal, they never mentioned it if he were pock-marked—scarred. It was no distinction. But if he didn't have the markings, they'd mention that!" He paused. "Those pock-marks weren't hereditary, but otherwise a blueskin is like a man who had them. He can't be anything else!"

"Then you think they're—human?"

"There's never yet been a case of reverse evolution," said Calhoun. "Maybe pithecanthropus had a monkey uncle, but no pithecanthropus ever went monkey."

She turned abruptly away. But she glanced at him often during that day. He continued to busy himself with those activities which make a Med Ship man's life consistent with retained sanity.

Next day she asked without preliminary;

"Don't you believe the blueskins planned for the ship with the dead men to arrive at Weald and spread plague there?"

"No," said Calhoun.

"Why?"

"It couldn't possibly work," Calhoun told her. "With only dead men on board, the ship wouldn't arrive at a place where the landing-grid could bring it down. So that would be no good. And plague-stricken living men wouldn't try to conceal that they had the plague. They might ask for help, but they'd know they'd instantly be killed on Weald if they were found to be plague-victims. So that would be no good, either! No, the ship wasn't intended to land plague on Weald."

"Are you—friendly to blueskins?" she asked uncertainly.

"Within reason," said Calhoun, "I am a well-wisher to all the human race. You're slipping, though. When using the word 'blueskin' you should say it uncomfortably, as if it were a word no refined person liked to pronounce. You don't. We'll land on Orede tomorrow, by the way. If you ever intend to tell me the truth, there's not much time."

She bit her lips. Twice, during the remainder of the day, she faced him and opened her mouth as if to speak, and then turned away again. Calhoun shrugged. He had fairly definite ideas about her, by now. He carefully kept them tentative, but no girl born and raised on Weald would willingly go to Orede, with all of Weald believing that a shipload of miners preferred death to remaining there. It tied in, like everything else that was unpleasant, to blueskins. Nobody from Weald would dream of landing on Orede! Not now!

A little before the Med Ship was due to break out from overdrive, the girl said very carefully;

"You've been—very kind. I'd like to thank you. I—didn't really believe I would—live to get to Orede."

Calhoun raised his eyebrows.

"I—wish I could tell you everything you want to know," she added regretfully. "I think you're—really decent. But some things…"

Calhoun said caustically;

"You've told me a great deal. You weren't born on Weald. You weren't raised there. The people of Dara—notice that I don't say blueskins, though they are—the people of Dara have made at least one space-ship since Weald threatened them with extermination. There probably a new food-shortage on Dara now, leading to pure desperation. Most likely it's bad enough to make them risk landing on Orede to kill cattle and freeze beef to help. They've worked out."

She gasped and sprang to her feet. She snatched out the tiny blaster in her pocket. She pointed it waveringly at him.

"I—have to kill you!" she cried desperately. "I—I have to!"

Calhoun reached out. She tugged despairingly at the blaster's trigger. Nothing happened. Before she could realize that she hadn't turned off the safety, Calhoun twisted the weapon from her fingers. He stepped back.

"Good girl!" he said approvingly. "I'll give this back to you when we land. And thanks. Thanks very much!"

She stared at him. "Thanks? When I tried to kill you?"

"Of course!" said Calhoun. "I'd made guesses. I couldn't know that they were right. When you tried to kill me, you confirmed every one. Now, when we land on Orede I'm going to get you to try to put me in touch with your friends. It's going to be tricky, because they must be pretty well scared about that ship. But it's a highly desirable thing to get done!"

He went to the ship's control-board and sat down before it.

"Twenty minutes to break-hour," he observed.

Murgatroyd peered out of his little cubbyhole. His eyes were anxious. *Tormals* are amiable little creatures. During the days in overdrive, Calhoun had paid less than the usual amount of attention to Murgatroyd, while the girl was fascinating. They'd made friends, awkwardly on the girl's part, very pleasantly on Murgatroyd's. But only moments ago there had been bitter emotion in the air. Murgatroyd had fled to his cubbyhole to escape it. He was distressed. Now that there was silence again, he peered out unhappily.

"*Chee?*" he queried plaintively. "*Chee-chee-chee?*"

Calhoun said matter-of-factly;

"It's all right, Murgatroyd. If we aren't blasted as we try to land, we should be able to make friends with everybody and get something accomplished."

The statement was hopelessly inaccurate.

CHAPTER THREE

There was no answer from the ground when breakout came and Calhoun drove the Med Ship to a favorable position for a call. He patiently repeated, over and over again, that Med Ship Aesclipus Twenty notified its arrival and requested coördinates for landing. There should have been a crisp description of the direction from the planet's center at which, a certain time so many hours or minutes later, the force-fields of the grid would find it convenient to lock onto and lower the Med Ship. But the communicator remained silent.

"There is a landing-grid," said Calhoun, frowning, "and if they're using it to load fresh meat for Dara, from the herds I'm told about, it should be manned. But they don't seem to intend to answer. Maybe they think that if they pretend I'm not here I'll go away."

He reflected, and his frown deepened.

"If I didn't know what I do know, I might. So if I land on emergency-rockets the blueskins down below may decide that I come from Weald. And in that case it would be reasonable to blast me before I could land and unload some fighting men. On the other hand, no ship from Weald would conceivably land without impassioned assurance that it was safe. It would drop bombs." He turned to the girl. "How many Darians down below?"

She shook her head.

"You don't know," said Calhoun, "or won't tell, yet. But they ought to be told about the arrival of that ship at Weald, and what Weald thinks about it! My guess is that you came to tell them. It isn't likely that Dara gets news direct from Weald. Where were you put ashore from Dara, when you set out to be a spy?"

Her lips parted to speak. But she compressed them tightly. She shook her head again.

"It must have been plenty far away," said Calhoun restlessly. "Your people would have built a ship, and made fine forged papers for it, and they'd travel so far from this part of space that when they landed nobody would think of Dara. They'd use makeup to cover the blue spots, but maybe it was so far away that blueskins had never been heard of!"

Her face looked pinched, but she did not reply.

"Then they'd land half a dozen of you, with a supply of makeup for the blue patches. And you'd separate, and take ships that went various roundabout ways, and arrive on Weald one by one, to see what could be done there to..." He stopped. "When did you find out positively that there wasn't any plague any more?"

She began to grow pale.

"I'm not a mind-reader," said Calhoun. "But it adds up. You're from Dara. You've been on Weald. It's practically certain that there are other, agents, if you like that word better, on Weald. And there hasn't been a plague on Weald so you people aren't carriers of it. But you knew it in advance, I think. How'd you learn? Did a ship in some sort of trouble land there, on Dara?"

"Y-yes," said the girl. "We wouldn't let it go again. But the people didn't catch—they didn't die—they lived—"

She stopped short.

"It's not fair to trap me!" she cried passionately, "It's not fair!"

"I'll stop," said Calhoun.

He turned to the control-board. The Med Ship was only planetary diameters from Orede, now, and the electron telescope showed shining stars in leisurely motion across its screen. Then a huge, gibbous shining shape appeared, and there were irregular patches of that muddy color which is sea-

123

bottom, and varicolored areas which were plains and forests. Also there were mountains. Calhoun steadied the image and squinted at it.

"The mine," he observed, "was found by members of a hunting-party, killing wild cattle for sport."

Even a small planet has many millions of square miles of surface, and a single human installation on a whole world will not be easy to find by random search. But there were clues to this one. Men hunting for sport would not choose a tropic nor an arctic climate to hunt in. So if they found a mineral deposit, it would have been in a temperate zone. Cattle would not be found deep in a mountainous terrain. The mine would not be on a prairie. The settlement on Orede, then, would be near the edge of mountains, not far from a prairie such as wild cattle would frequent, and it would be in a temperate climate. Forested areas could be ruled out. And there would be a landing-grid. Handling only one ship at a time, it might be a very small grid. It need be only hundreds of yards across and less than half a mile high. But its shadow would be distinctive.

Calhoun searched among low mountains near unforested prairie in a temperate zone. He found a speck. He enlarged it many-fold, and it was the mine on Orede. There were heaps of tailings. There was something which cast a long, lacy shadow. The landing-grid.

"But they don't answer our call," observed Calhoun, "so we go down unwelcomed."

He inverted the Med Ship and the emergency-rockets boomed. The ship plunged planetward.

A long time later it was deep in the planet's atmosphere. The noise of its rockets had become thunderous, with air to carry and to reinforce the sound.

"Hold on to something, Murgatroyd," commanded Calhoun. "We may have to dodge some ack."

But nothing came up from below. The Med Ship again inverted itself, and its rockets pointed toward the planet and poured out pencil-thin, blue-white, high-velocity flames. It checked slightly, but continued to descend. It was not directly above the grid. It swept downward until almost level with the peaks of the mountains in which the mine lay. It tilted again, and swept onward over the mountain-tops, and then tilted once more and went racing up the valley in which the landing-grid was plainly visible. Calhoun swung it on an erratic course, lest there be opposition.

But there was no sign. Then the rockets bellowed, and the ship slowed its forward motion, hovered momentarily, and settled to solidity outside the framework of the grid. The grid was small, as Calhoun reasoned. But it reached interminably toward the sky.

The rocket cut off. Slender as the flame had been, they'd melted and bored thin drill-holes deep into the soil. Molten rock boiled and bubbled down below. But there seemed no other sound. There was no other motion. There was absolute stillness all around. But when Calhoun switched on the outside microphones a faint, sweet melange of high-pitched chirpings came from tiny creatures hidden under the vegetation of the mountainsides.

Calhoun put a blaster in his pocket and stood up.

"We'll see what it looks like outside," he said with a certain grimness. "I don't quite believe what the visionscreens show."

Minutes later he stepped down to the ground from the Med Ship's exit-port. The ship had landed perhaps a hundred feet from what once had been a wooden building. In it, ore from the mines was concentrated and the useless tailings carried away by a conveyor-belt to make a monstrous pile of broken stone. But there was no longer a building. Next to it there had been a structure containing an ore-crusher. The massive machinery could still be seen, but the structure was fragments. Next to that, again, had been the shaft-head shelters of the mine. They also were shattered practically to match-sticks.

The look of the ground about the building-sites was simply and purely impossible. It was a mass of hoofprints. Cattle by thousands and tens of thousands had trampled everything. Cattle had burst in the wooden sides of the buildings. Cattle had piled themselves up against the beams upholding roofs until the buildings collapsed. Then cattle had gone plunging over the wrecked buildings until there was nothing left but indescribable chaos. Many, many cattle had died in the crush. There were heaps of dead beasts about the metal girders which were the foundation of the landing-grid. The air was tainted by the smell of carrion.

The settlement had been destroyed, positively, by stampeded cattle in tens or hundreds of thousands charging blindly through and over and upon it. Senselessly, they'd trampled each other to horrible shapelessnesses. The mine-shaft was not choked, because enormously strong timbers had fallen across and blocked it. But everything else was pure destruction.

Calhoun said evenly;

"Clever! Very clever! You can't blame men when beasts stampede! We should accept the evidence that some monstrous herd, making its way through a mountain pass, somehow went crazy and bolted for the plains and this settlement got in the way and it was too bad for the settlement. Everything's explained, except the ship that went to Weald. A cattle stampede, yes. Anybody can believe that! But there was a man-stampede! Men stampeded into the ship as blindly as the cattle trampled down this little town. The ship stampeded off into space as insanely as the cattle. But a stampede of men *and* cattle, in the same place,—that's a little too much at one time!"

"How," asked Calhoun directly, "do you intend to get in touch with your friends here?"

"I—I don't know," she said distressedly. "But if—the ship stays here, they're bound to come and see why. Won't they? Or will they?"

"If they're sane, they won't," said Calhoun. "The one undesirable thing, here, would be human footprints on top of cattle-tracks. If your friends are a meat-getting party from Dara, as I believe, they should cover up their tracks, get off-planet as fast as possible, and pray that no signs of their former presence are ever discovered. That would be their best first move, certainly!"

"What should I do?" she asked helplessly.

"I'm far from sure. At a guess, and for the moment, probably nothing. I'll work something out... I've got the devil of a job before me, though. I can't spend too much time here."

"You can—leave me here..."

He grunted and turned away. It was naturally unthinkable that he should leave another human being on a supposedly uninhabited planet, with the knowledge that it might actually be uninhabited, and the further knowledge that any visitors would have the strongest of possible reasons to hide themselves away.

He believed that there were Darians here, and the girl in the Med ship—so he also believed—was a Darian. But any who might be hiding had so much to lose if they were discovered that they might be hundreds or even thousands of miles from anywhere a space-ship would normally land—if they hadn't fled after the incident of the space-ship's departure with its load of doomed passengers.

Considered detachedly, the odds were that there was again a food-shortage on Dara. That blueskins, in desperation, had raided or were raiding or would raid the cattle-herds of Orede for food to carry back to their home planet. That somehow the miners on Orede had found that they had blueskin neighbors, and died of the consequences of their terror. It was a risky guess to make on such evidence as Calhoun considered he had, but no other guess was possible.

If his guess was right, he was under some obligation to do exactly what he believed the girl considered her mission, to warn all blueskins that Weald would presently try to find them on Orede, when all hell must break loose upon Dara for punishment. But if there were men here, he couldn't leave a written warning for them in default of friendly contact. They might not find it, and a search-party of Wealdians might. All he could possibly do was try to make contact and give warning by such means as would leave no evidence behind that he'd done so. Weald would consider a warning sure proof of blueskin guilt.

It was not satisfactory to be limited to broadcasts which might not be picked up, and were unlikely to be acknowledged. But he settled down with the communicator to make the attempt.

He called first on a GC wave-length and form. It was unlikely that blueskins would use general-communication bands to keep in touch with each other, but it had to be tried. He broadcast, as broadly tuned as possible, and went up and down the GC spectrum, repeating his warning painstakingly and listening without hope for a reply. He did find one spot on the dial where there was re-radiation of his message, as if from a tuned receiver. But he could not get a fix on it, and nobody might be listening. He exhausted the normal communication pattern. Then he broadcast on old-fashioned amplitude modulation which a modern communicator would not pick up at all, and which therefore might be used by men in hiding.

He worked for a long time. Then he shrugged and gave it up. He'd repeated to absolute tedium the facts that any Darians—blueskins—on Orede ought to know. There'd been no answer. And it was all too likely that if he'd been received, that those who heard him took his message for a trick to discover if there were any hearers.

He clicked off at last and stood up, shaking his head. Suddenly the Med Ship seemed empty. Then he saw Murgatroyd staring at the exit-port. The inner door of that small airlock was closed. The tell-tale said the outer was not locked. Someone had gone out, quietly. The girl. Of course. Calhoun said angrily;

"How long ago, Murgatroyd?"

"*Chee!*" said Murgatroyd indignantly.

It wasn't an answer, but it showed that Murgatroyd was vexed that he'd been left behind. He and the girl were close friends, now. If she'd left Murgatroyd in the ship when he wanted to go with her, she wasn't coming back.

Calhoun swore. Then he made certain. She was not in the ship. He flipped the outside-speaker switch and said curtly into the microphone;

"Coffee! Murgatroyd and I are having coffee. Will you come back, please?"

He repeated the call, and repeated it again. Multiplied as his voice was by the speakers, she should hear him within a mile. She did not appear. He went to a small and inconspicuous closet and armed himself. A Med Ship man was not ever expected to fight, but there were blast-rifles available for extreme emergency.

When he'd slung a power-pack over his shoulder and reached the airlock, there was still no sign of his late stowaway. He stood in the airlock door for long minutes,

staring angrily about. Almost certainly she wouldn't be
looking in the mountains for men of Dara come here for
cattle. He used a pair of binoculars, first at low-magnification
to search as wide an area down-valley as possible, and then at
highest power to search the most likely routes.

He found a small, bobbing speck beyond a far-away
hillcrest. It was her head. It went down below the hilltop.

He snapped a command to Murgatroyd, and when the
tormal was on the ground outside, he locked the port with that
combination that nobody but a Med Ship man was at all likely
to discover or use.

"She's an idiot!" he told Murgatroyd sourly. "Come along!
We've got to be idiots too!"

He set out in pursuit.

The girl had a long start. Twice Calhoun came to places
where she could have chosen either of two ways onward.
Each time he had to determine which she'd followed. That
cost time. Then the mountains ended, abruptly, and a vast
undulating plain stretched away to the horizon. There were
at least two large masses and many smaller clumps of what
could only be animals gathered together. Cattle.

But here the girl was plainly in view. Calhoun increased
his stride. He began to gain on her. She did not look behind.

Murgatroyd said "*Chee!*" in a complaining tone.

"I should have left you behind," agreed Calhoun dourly,
"but there was and is a chance I won't get back. You'll have
to keep on hiking."

He plodded on. His memory of the terrain around the
mining settlement told him that there was no definite
destination in the girl's mind. But she was in no such despair
as to want deliberately to be lost. She'd guessed, Calhoun
believed, that if there were Darians on the planet, they'd keep
the landing-grid under observation. If they saw her leave that
area and could see that she was alone, they should intercept

her to find out the meaning of the Med Ship's landing. Then she could identify herself as one of them and give them the terribly necessary warning of Weald's suspicions.

"But," said Calhoun sourly, "if she's right, they'll have seen me marching after her now, which spoils her scheme. And I'd like to help it, but the way she's going is too dangerous!"

He went down into one of the hollows of the uneven plain. He saw a clump of a dozen or so cattle a little distance away. The bull looked up and snorted. The cows regarded him truculently. Their air was not one of bovine tranquility.

He was up the farther hillside and out of sight before the bull worked himself up to a charge. Then Calhoun suddenly remembered one of the items in the data about cattle he'd looked into just the other day. He felt himself grow pale.

"Murgatroyd!" he said sharply. "We've got to catch up! Fast! Stay with me if you can, but…" He was jog-trotting as he spoke—"even if you get lost I have to hurry!"

He ran fifty paces and walked fifty paces. He ran fifty and walked fifty. He saw her, atop a rolling of the ground. She came to a full stop. He ran. He saw her turn to retrace her steps. He flung to the safety of the blast-rifle and let off a roaring blast at the ground for her to hear.

Suddenly she was fleeing desperately, toward him. He plunged on. She vanished down into a hollow. Horns appeared over the hillcrest she'd just left. Cattle appeared. Four—a dozen—fifteen—twenty. They moved ominously in her wake. He saw her again, running frantically over another upward swell of the prairie. He let off another blast to guide her. He ran on at top speed with Murgatroyd trailing anxiously behind. From time to time Murgatroyd called "*Chee-chee-chee!*" in frightened pleading not to be abandoned.

More cattle appeared against the horizon. Fifty or a hundred. They came after the first clump. The first-seen group of a bull and his harem were moving faster, now. The girl fled from them, but it is the instinct of beef-cattle on the open range—Calhoun had learned it only two days before—to charge any human they find on foot. A mounted man to their dim minds is a creature to be tolerated or fled from, but a human on foot is to be crushed and stamped and gored.

Those in the lead were definitely charging now, with heads bent low. The bull charged furiously with shut eyes, as bulls do, but the many-times-more-deadly cows charged with their eyes wide open and wickedly alert, and with a lumbering speed much greater than the girl could manage.

She came up over the last rise, chalky-white and gasping, her hair flying, in the last extremity of terror. The nearest of the pursuing cattle were within ten yards when Calhoun fired from twenty yards beyond. One creature bellowed as the blast-bolt struck. It went down and others crashed into it and swept over it, and more came on. The girl saw Calhoun, now, and ran toward him, panting, and he knelt very deliberately and began to check the charge by shooting the leading animals.

He did not succeed. There were more cattle following the first, and more and more behind them. It appeared that all the cattle on the plain joined in the blind and senseless charge. The thudding of hooves became a mutter and then a rumble and then a growl. Plunging, clumsy figures rushed past on either side. But horns and heads heaved up over the mound of animals Calhoun had shot. He shot them too. More and more cattle came pounding past the rampart of his victims, but always, it seemed, some elected to climb the heap of their dead and dying fellows, and Calhoun shot and shot.

But he split the herd. The foremost animals had been charging a sighted human enemy. Others had followed because it is the instinct of cattle to join their running fellows in whatever crazed urgency they feel. There was a dense, pounding, horrible mass of running bulls and cows and calves; bellowing, wailing, grunting, puffing, raising thick and impenetrable clouds of dust which had everything but galloping beasts going past on either side.

It lasted for minutes. Then the thunder of hooves diminished. It ended abruptly, and Calhoun and the girl were left alone with the gruesome pile of animals which had divided the charging herd into two parts. They could see the rears of innumerable running animals, stupidly continuing the charge—hardly different, now, from a stampede—whose original objective none now remembered.

Calhoun thoughtfully touched the barrel of his blast-rifle and winced at its scorching heat.

"I just realized," he said coldly, "that I don't know your name. What is it?"

"M-maril," said the girl. She swallowed hard. "Th-thank you—"

"Maril," said Calhoun, "you are an idiot! It was half-witted at best to go off by yourself! You could have been lost! You could have cost me days of hunting for you, days badly needed for more important matters!" He stopped and took breath. "You may have spoiled what little chance I've got to do something about the plans Weald's already making!"

He said more bitterly still;

"And I had to leave Murgatroyd behind to get to you in time! He was right in the path of that charge!"

He turned away from her and said dourly;

"All right! Come on back to the ship. We'll go to Dara. We'd have to, anyhow. But Murgatroyd—"

Then he heard a very small sneeze. Out of a rolling wall of still-roiling dust, Murgatroyd appeared forlornly. He was dust-covered, and draggled, and his tail drooped, and he sneezed again. He moved as if he could barely put one paw before another, but at the sight of Calhoun he sneezed yet again and said, "*Chee!*" in a disconsolate voice. Then he sat down and waited for Calhoun to pick him up.

When Calhoun did so, Murgatroyd clung to him pathetically and said, "*Chee-chee!*" and again "*Chee-chee!*" with the intonation of one telling of incredible horrors and disasters endured.

Calhoun headed back for the valley, the settlement and the Med Ship. Murgatroyd clung to his neck. The girl Maril followed visibly shaken.

Calhoun did not speak to her again. He led the way. A mile back toward the mountains, they began to see stragglers from the now-vanished herd. A little further, those stragglers began to notice them. And it would have been a matter of no moment if they'd been domesticated dairy-cattle, but these were range-cattle gone wild. Twice, Calhoun had to use his blast-rifle to discourage incipient charges by irritated bulls or even more irritated cows. Those with calves darkly suspected Calhoun of designs upon their offspring.

It was a relief to enter the valley again. But it was two miles more to the landing-grid with the Med Ship beside it and the reek of carrion in the air.

They were perhaps two hundred feet from the ship when a blast-rifle crashed and its bolt whined past Calhoun so close that he felt the monstrous heat. There had been no challenge. There was no warning. There was simply a shot which came horribly close to ending Calhoun's career in a completely arbitrary fashion.

CHAPTER FOUR

Five minutes later Calhoun had located one would-be killer behind a mass of splintered planking that once had been a wall. He set the wood afire by a blaster-bolt and then viciously sent other bolts all around the man it had sheltered when he fled from the flames. He could have killed him ten times over, but it was more desirable to open communication. So he missed, intentionally.

Maril had cried out that she came from Dara and had word for them, but they did not answer. There were three men with heavy-duty blast-rifles. One was the one Calhoun had burned out of his hiding-place. That man's rifle exploded when the flames hit it. Two remained. One—so Calhoun presently discovered—was working his way behind underbrush to a shelf from which he could shoot down at Calhoun. Calhoun had dropped into a hollow and pulled Maril to cover at the first shot. The second man happily planned to get to a point where he could shoot him like a fish in a barrel. The third man had fired half a dozen times and then disappeared. Calhoun estimated that he intended to get around to the rear, in hope there was no protection from that direction for Calhoun. It would take some time for him to manage it.

So Calhoun industriously concentrated his fire on the man trying to get above him. He was behind a boulder, not too dissimilar to Calhoun's breastwork. Calhoun set fire to the brush at the point at which the other man aimed. That, then, made his effort useless. Then Calhoun sent a dozen bolts at the other man's rocky shield. It heated up. Steam rose in a whitish mass and blew directly away from Calhoun. He saw that antagonist flee. He saw him so clearly that he was positive that there was a patch of blue pigment on the right-hand side of the back of his neck.

He grunted and swung to find the third. That man moved through thick undergrowth, and Calhoun set it on fire in a neat pattern of spreading flames. Evidently, these men had had no training in battle-tactics with blast-rifles. The third man also had to get away. He did. But something from him arched through the smoke. It fell to the ground directly upwind from Calhoun. White smoke puffed up violently.

It was instinct that made Calhoun react as he did. He jerked the girl Maril to her feet and rushed her toward the Med Ship. Smoke from the flung bomb upwind barely swirled around him and missed Maril altogether. Calhoun, though, got a whiff of something strange, not scorched or burning vegetation at all. He ceased to breathe and plunged onward. In clear air he emptied his lungs and refilled them. They were then halfway to the ship, with Murgatroyd prancing on ahead.

But then Calhoun's heart began to pound furiously. His muscles twitched and tense. He felt extraordinary symptoms like an extreme of agitation. Calhoun was familiar enough with tear-gas, used by police on some planets. But this was different and worse. Even as he helped and urged Maril onward, he automatically considered his sensations, and had it. Panic gas! Police did not use it because panic is worse than rioting. Calhoun felt all the physical symptoms of fear and of gibbering terror. A man whose mind yields to terror experiences certain physical sensations, wildly beating heart, tensed and twitching muscles, and a frantic impulse to convulsive action. A man in whom those physical sensations are induced by other means will—ordinarily—find his mind yielding to terror.

Calhoun couldn't combat his feelings, but his clinical attitude enabled him to act despite them. The three from Weald reached the base of the Med Ship. One of their enemies had lost his rifle and need not be counted. Another had fled from flames and might be ignored for some moments, anyhow. But a blast-bolt struck the ship's metal hull only feet from Calhoun, and he whipped around to the other side and let loose a staccato of fire which emptied the rifle of all its charges.

Then he opened the airlock door, hating the fact that he shook and trembled. He urged the girl and Murgatroyd in. He slammed the outer airlock door just as another blaster-bolt hit.

"They—they don't realize," said Maril desperately. "If they only knew—"

"Talk to them, if you like," said Calhoun. His teeth chattered and he raged, because the symptom was of terror he denied.

He pushed a button on the control-board. He pointed to a microphone. He got at an oxygen-bottle and inhaled deeply. Oxygen, obviously, should be an antidote for panic, since the symptoms of terror act to increase the oxygenation of the blood-stream and muscles, and to make superhuman exertion possible if necessary. Breathing ninety-five per cent oxygen produced the effect the terror-inspiring gas strove for, so his heart slowed nearly to normal and his body relaxed. He held out his hand and it did not tremble.

He turned to Maril. She hadn't spoken into the mike yet.

"They—may not be from Dara!" she said shakily. "I just thought! They could be somebody else—maybe criminals who planned to raid the mine for a shipload of its ore…"

"Nonsense!" said Calhoun. "I saw one of them clearly enough to be sure. But they're skeptical characters. I'm afraid there may be more on the way here wherever they keep themselves. Anyhow, now we know some of them are in hearing! I'll take advantage of that and we'll go on."

He took the microphone. Instants later his voice boomed in the stillness outside the ship, cutting through the thin shrill of invisible small creatures.

"This is the Med Ship Aesclipus Twenty," said Calhoun's voice, amplified to a shout. "I left Weald four days ago, one day after the cargo-ship from here arrived with everybody on board dead. On Weald they don't know how it happened, but they suspect blueskins. Sooner or later they'll search here. Get away! Cover up your tracks! Hide all signs that you've ever been here! Get the hell away, fast! One more warning! There's talk of fusion-bombing Dara. They're scared! If they find your traces, they'll be more scared still! So cover up your tracks and—get—away—from—here!"

The many-times-multiplied voice rolled and echoed among the hills. But it was very clear. Where it could be heard it could be understood, and it could be heard for miles.

But there was no response to it. Calhoun waited a reasonable time. Then he shrugged and seated himself at the control-board.

"It isn't easy," he observed, "to persuade desperate men that they've out-smarted themselves! Hold hard, Murgatroyd!"

The rockets bellowed. Then there was a tremendous noise to end all noises, and the ship began to climb. It sped up and up and up. By the time it was out of atmosphere it had velocity enough to coast to clear space and Calhoun cut the rockets altogether. He busied himself with those astrogational chores which began with orienting oneself to galactic directions after leaving a planet which rotates at its own individual speed. Then one computes the overdrive course to another planet, from the respective coördinates of the world one is leaving and the one one aims for. Then,—in this case at any rate—there was the very finicky task of picking out a fourth-magnitude star of whose planets one was his destination. He aimed for it with ultra-fine precision.

"Overdrive coming," he said presently. "Hold on!"

Space reeled. There was nausea and giddiness and a horrible sensation of falling in a wildly unlikely spiral. Then stillness, and solidity, and the blackness of the Pit outside the Med Ship. The little craft was in overdrive again.

After a long while, the girl Maril said uneasily.

"I don't know what you plan now—"

"I'm going to Dara," said Calhoun. "On Orede I tried to get the blueskins there to get going, fast. Maybe I succeeded. I don't know. But this thing's been mishandled! Even if there's a famine, people shouldn't do things out of desperation!"

"I know now that I was—very foolish—"

"Forget it," commanded Calhoun. "I wasn't talking about you. Here I run into a situation that the Med Service should have caught and cleaned up generations ago! But it's not only a Med Service obligation, it's a current mess! Before I could begin to get at the basic problem, those idiots on Orede— It'd happened before I reached Weald! An emotional explosion triggered by a ship full of dead men that nobody intended to kill."

Maril shook her head.

"Those Darian characters," said Calhoun annoyedly, "shouldn't have gone to Orede in the first place. If they went there, they should at least have stayed on a continent where there were no people from Weald digging a mine and hunting cattle for sport on their off days! They could be spotted! I believe they were! And again, if it had been a long way from the mine installation, they could probably have wiped out the people who sighted them before they could get back with the news! But it looks like miners saw men hunting, and got close enough to see they were blueskins, and then got back to the mine with the news!"

She waited for him to explain.

"I know I'm guessing, but it fits!" he said distastefully. "So something had to be done. Either the mining settlement had to be wiped out or the story that blueskins were on Orede had to be discredited. The blueskins tried for both. They used panic-gas on a herd of cattle and it made them

crazy and they charged the settlement like the four-footed
lunatics they are! And the blueskins used panic-gas on the
settlement itself as the cattle went through. It should have
settled the whole business nicely. After it was over every man
in the settlement would believe he'd been out of his head for
a while, and he'd have the crazy state of the settlement to
think about, and he wouldn't be sure of what he'd seen or
heard beforehand. They might try to verify the blueskin story
later, but they wouldn't believe anything certainly! It should
have worked!"

Again she waited. So Calhoun said very wrily indeed;

"Unfortunately, when the miners panicked, they
stampeded into the ship. Also unfortunately, panic-gas got
into the ship with them. So they stayed panicked while the
astrogator—in panic!—took off and headed for Weald and
threw on the overdrive—which would be set for Weald
anyhow—because that would be the fastest way to run away
from whatever he imagined he feared. But he and all the men
on the ship were still crazy with panic from the gas they were
re-breathing until they died!"

Silence. After a long interval, Maril asked;

"You don't think the—Darians intended to kill?"

"I think they were stupid!" said Calhoun angrily.
"Somebody's always urging the police to use panic-gas in case
of public tumult. But it's too dangerous. Nobody knows
what one man will do in a panic. Take a hundred or two or
three and panic them all, and there's no limit to their
craziness! The whole thing was handled wrong!"

"But you don't blame them?"

"For being stupid, yes," said Calhoun fretfully. "But if I'd
been in their place, perhaps…"

"Where were you born?" asked Maril suddenly.

Calhoun jerked his head around. He said;

"No! Not where you're guessing—or hoping. Not on Dara. Just because I act as if Darians were human doesn't mean I have to be one! I'm a Med Service man, and I'm acting as I think I should." His tone became exasperated. "Dammit, I'm supposed to deal with health situations, actual and possible causes of human deaths! And if Weald thinks it finds proof that blueskins are in space again and caused the death of Wealdians it won't be healthy! They're halfway set anyhow to drop fusion-bombs on Dara to wipe it out!"

Maril said fiercely;

"They might as well drop bombs. It'll be quicker than starvation, at least!"

Calhoun looked at her more exasperatedly than before.

"It is a crop failure again?" he demanded. When she nodded he said bitterly; "Famine conditions already?" When she nodded again he said drearily; "And of course famine is the great-grandfather of health problems! And that's right in my lap with all the rest!"

He stood up. Then he sat down again.

"I'm tired!" he said flatly. "I'd like to get some sleep."

Maril understood. She picked up a book and went into the other cabin.

Alone in the control compartment, he tried to relax, but it was not possible. He flung himself into a comfortable chair and considered the situation of the people of the planet Dara. Those people were marked by patches of blue pigment as an inherited consequence of a plague of three generations past. Dara was a planet of pariahs, excluded from the human race by those who had been conditioned to fear them.

And now there was famine on Dara for the second time, and they were of no mind to starve quietly. There was food on the planet Orede, monstrous herds of cattle without owners. It was natural enough for Darians to build a ship or ships and try to bring food back to its starving people. But that desperately necessary enterprise had now roused Weald to a frenzy of apprehension. Weald was if possible more hysterically afraid of blueskins than ever before, and even more implacably the enemy of the starving planet's population. Weald itself throve and prospered. Ironically, it had such an excess of foodstuffs that it stored them in unneeded space-ships in orbits about itself. Hundreds of thousands of tons of grain circled Weald in sealed-tight hulks, while the people of Dara starved and only dared try to steal—it could be called stealing—some of the innumerable wild cattle of Orede.

The blueskins on Orede could not trust Calhoun, so they pretended not to hear—or maybe they didn't hear. They'd been abandoned and betrayed by all of humanity beyond their world. They'd been threatened and oppressed by guardships in orbit about them, ready to shoot down any space-craft they might send aloft.

So Calhoun pondered…

A long time later Calhoun heard small sounds which were not normal on a Med Ship in overdrive. They were not part of the random noises carefully generated to keep the silence of the ship endurable. Calhoun raised his head. He listened sharply. No sound could come from outside.

He knocked on the door of the sleeping-cabin. The noises stopped instantly.

"Come out," he commanded through the door.

"I'm—I'm all right," said Maril's voice. But it was not quite steady. She paused. "I was just having a bad dream."

"I wish," said Calhoun, "that you'd tell me the truth occasionally! Come out, please!"

There were stirrings. After a little the door opened and Maril appeared. She looked as if she'd been crying. She said quickly;

"I probably look queer, but it's because I was asleep."

"To the contrary," said Calhoun, fuming, "you've been lying awake crying. I don't know why. I've been out here wishing I could sleep, because I'm frustrated. But since you aren't asleep maybe you can help me with my job. I've figured some things out. For some others I need facts. How about it?"

She swallowed.

"I'll try."

"Coffee?" he asked.

Murgatroyd popped his head out of his miniature sleeping-cabin.

"*Chee?*" he asked interestedly.

"Go back to sleep!" snapped Calhoun.

He began to pace back and forth.

"I need to know something about the pigment patches," he said jerkily. "Maybe it sounds crazy to think of such things now. First things first, you know. But that is a first thing! So long as Darians don't look like the people of other worlds, they'll be considered different. If they look repulsive, they'll be thought of as evil... Tell me about those patches. They're different-sized and different-shaped and they appear in different places. You've none on your face or hands, anyhow."

"I haven't any at all," said the girl reservedly.

"I thought—"

"Not everybody," she said defensively. "Nearly, yes. But not all. Some people don't have them. Some people are born with bluish splotches on their skin, but they fade out while they're children. When they grow up they're just like—the people of Weald or any other world. And their children never have them."

Calhoun stared.

"You couldn't possibly be proved to be a Darian, then?"

She shook her head. Calhoun remembered, and started the coffee-maker.

"When you left Dara," he said, "You were carried a long, long way, to some planet where they'd practically never heard of Dara, and where the name meant nothing. You could have settled there, or anywhere else and forgotten about Dara. But you didn't. Why not, since you're not a blueskin?"

"But I am!" she said fiercely. "My parents, my brothers and sisters, and Korvan—"

Then she bit her lip. Calhoun took note but did not comment on the name that she had mentioned.

"Then your parents had the splotches fade, so you never had them," he said absorbedly. "Something like that happened on Tralee, once! There's a virus—a whole group of virus particles! Normally we humans are immune to them. One has to be in terrifically bad physical condition for them to take hold and produce whatever effects they do. But once they're established they're passed on from mother to child... And when they die out it's during childhood, too!"

He poured coffee for the two of them. As usual, Murgatroyd swung down to the floor and said impatiently;

"*Chee! Chee! Chee!*"

Calhoun absently filled Murgatroyd's tiny cup and handed it to him.

"But this is marvellous!" he said exuberantly. "The blue patches appeared after the plague, didn't they? After people recovered—when they recovered?"

Maril stared at him. His mind was filled with strictly professional considerations. He was not talking to her as a person. She was purely a source of information.

"So I'm told," said Maril reservedly. "Are there any more humiliating questions you want to ask?"

He gaped at her. Then he said ruefully;

"I'm stupid, Maril, but you're touchy. There's nothing personal."

"There is to me!" she said fiercely. "I was born among blueskins, and they're of my blood, and they're hated and I'd have been killed on Weald if I'd been known as—what I am! And there's Korvan, who arranged for me to be sent away as a spy and advised me to do just what you said,—abandon my home world and everybody I care about! Including him! It's personal to me!"

Calhoun wrinkled his forehead helplessly.

"I'm sorry," he repeated, "Drink your coffee!"

"I don't want it," she said bitterly. "I'd like to die!"

"If you stay around where I am," Calhoun told her, "you may get your wish. All right. There'll be no more questions, I promise."

She turned and moved toward the door to the sleeping-cabin. Calhoun looked after her.

"Maril," he called out to her.

"What?"

"Why were you crying?"

"You wouldn't understand," she said evenly.

Calhoun shrugged his shoulders almost up to his ears. He was a professional man. In his profession he was not incompetent. But there is no profession in which a really competent man tries to understand women. Calhoun annoyedly had to let fate or chance or disaster take care of Maril's personal problems. He had larger matters to cope with.

But he had something to work on, now. He hunted busily in the reference tapes. He came up with an explicit collection of information on exactly the subject he needed. He left the control-room to go down into the storage areas of the Med Ship's hull. He found an ultra-frigid storage box, whose contents were kept at the temperature of liquid air. He donned thick gloves, used a special set of tongs, and extracted a tiny block of plastic in which a sealed-tight phial of glass was embedded. It frosted instantly he took it out, and when the storage-box was closed again the block was covered with a thick and opaque coating of frozen moisture.

He went back to the control-room and pulled down the panel which made available a small-scale but surprisingly adequate biological laboratory. He set the plastic block in a container which would raise it very, very gradually to a specific temperature and hold it there. It was, obviously, a living culture from which any imaginable quantity of the same culture could be bred. Calhoun set the apparatus with great exactitude.

"This," he told Murgatroyd, "may be a good day's work. Now I think I can rest."

Then, for a long while, there was no sound or movement in the Med Ship. The girl Maril may have slept, or maybe not. Calhoun lay relaxed in a chair which at the touch of a button became the most comfortable of sleeping-places. Murgatroyd remained in his cubbyhole, his tail curled over his nose. There were comforting, unheard, easily dismissable murmurings now and again. They kept the feeling of life alive in the ship. But for such infinitesimal stirrings of sound—carefully recorded for this exact purpose—the feel of the ship would have been that of a tomb.

But it was quite otherwise when another ship-day began with the taped sounds of morning activities as faint as echoes but nevertheless establishing an atmosphere of their own.

Calhoun examined the plastic block and its contents. He read the instruments which had cared for it while he slept. He put the block—no longer frosted—in the culture-microscope and saw its enclosed, infinitesimal particles of life in the process of multiplying on the food that had been frozen with them when they were reduced to the spore condition. He beamed. He replaced the block in the incubation oven and faced the day cheerfully.

Maril greeted him with great reserve. They breakfasted.

"I've been thinking," said Maril evenly. "I think I can get you a hearing for—whatever ideas you may have to help Dara."

"Kind of you," murmured Calhoun. "May I ask whose influence you'll exert?"

"There's a man," said Maril reservedly, "who—thinks a great deal of me. I don't know his present official position, but he was certain to become prominent. I'll tell him how you've acted up to now, and your attitude, and of course that you're Med Service. He'll be glad to help you, I'm sure."

"Splendid!" said Calhoun, nodding. "That will be Korvan."

She started.

"How did you know?"

"Intuition," said Calhoun drily. "All right. I'll count on him."

But he did not. He worked in the tiny biological lab all that ship-day and all the next. The girl remained quiet.

On the ship-day after, the time for breakfast approached. And while the ship was practically a world all by itself, it was easy to look forward with confidence to the future. But when contact and—in a fashion—conflict with other and larger worlds loomed nearer, prospects seemed less bright. Calhoun had definite plans, now, but there were so many ways in which they could be frustrated! Weald's political leaders could not oppose hysterical demands for action against blueskins, after a deathship arrived with no signs whatever of blueskins as responsible for its cargo of corpses. It was certain that a starving Dara would tend to desperate and fatal measures against hereditary enemies.

PARIAH PLANET

Calhoun sat down at the control-board and watched the clock.

"I've got things lined up," he told Maril wrily, "if only they work out. *If* I can make somebody on Dara listen and follow my advice and *if* Weald doesn't get ideas and isn't doing what I suspect it is, maybe something can be done."

"I'm sure you'll do your best," said Maril politely.

Calhoun managed to grin. He watched the ship-clock. There was no sensation attached to overdrive travel except at the beginning and the end. It was now time for the end. He might find that absolutely anything had happened while he made plans which would immediately be seen to be hopeless. Weald could have sent ships to Dara, or Dara might be in such a state of desperation that...

As it turned out, Dara was desperate. The Med Ship came out nearly a light-month from the sun about which the planet Dara revolved. Calhoun went into a short hop toward it. Then Dara was on the other side of the blazing yellow star. It took time to reach it. He called down, identifying himself and the ship and asking for coördinates so his ship could be brought to ground. There was confusion, as if the request were so unusual that the answers were not ready. The grid, too, was on the planet's night side. Presently the ship was locked onto by the grid's force-fields. It went downward without incident.

Calhoun saw that Maril sat tensely, twisting her fingers within each other, until the ship actually touched ground.

Then he opened the exit-port, and faced armed men in the darkness, with blast-rifles trained on him. There was a portable cannon trained on the Med Ship itself.

"Come out!" rasped a voice. "If you try anything you get blasted! Your ship and its contents are seized by the planetary government!"

CHAPTER FIVE

It seemed that the smell of hunger was in the air. The armed men were cadaverous. Lights came on, and stark, harsh shadows lay black upon the ground. Calhoun's captors were uniformed, but the uniforms hung loosely upon them. Where the lights struck upon their faces, their cheeks were hollow. They were emaciated. And there were the splotches of pigment of which Calhoun had heard. The leader of the truculent group was blue, except for two fingers which in the glaring illumination seemed whiter than white.

"Out!" said that man savagely. "We're taking over your stock of food. You'll get your share of it, like everybody else, but—out!"

Maril spoke over Calhoun's shoulder. She uttered a cryptic sentence or two. It should have amounted to identification, but there was skepticism in the the armed party.

"Oh, you're one of us, eh?" said the guard-leader sardonically. "You'll have a chance to prove that! Come out of there!"

Calhoun spoke abruptly;

"This is a Med Ship," he said. "There are medicines and bacterial cultures, inside it. They shouldn't be meddled with. Here on Dara you've had enough of plagues!"

The man with the blue hand said as sardonically as before;

"I said the government was taking over your ship! It won't be looted. But you're not taking a full cargo of food away! In fact, it's not likely you're leaving!"

"I want to speak to someone in authority," snapped Calhoun. "We've just come from Weald." He felt bristling hatred all about him as he named Weald. "There's tumult there. They're talking about dropping fusion bombs here.

It's important that I talk to somebody with the authority to take a few sensible precautions!"

He descended to the ground. There was a panicky "*Chee! Chee!*" from behind him, and Murgatroyd came dashing to swarm up his body and cling apprehensively to his neck.

"What's that?"

"A *tormal,*" said Calhoun. "He's not a pet. Your medical men will know something about him. This is a Med Ship and I'm a Med Ship man, and he's an important member of the crew. He's a Med Ship *tormal* and he stays with me!"

The man with the blue hand said harshly;

"There's somebody waiting to ask you questions. Here!"

A ground-car came rolling out from the side of the landing-grid enclosure. The ground-car ran on wheels, and wheels were not much used on modern worlds. Dara was behind the times in more ways than one.

"This car will take you to Defense and you can tell them anything you want. But don't try to sneak back in this ship! It'll be guarded!"

The ground-car was enclosed, with room for a driver and the three from the Med Ship. But armed men festooned themselves about its exterior and it went bumping and rolling to the massive ground-layer girders of the grid. It rolled out under them and there was paved highway. It picked up speed.

There were buildings on either side of the road, but few showed lights. This was night-time, and the men at the landing-grid had set a pattern of hunger, so that the silence and the dark buildings did not seem a sign of tranquility and sleep, but of exhaustion and despair. The highway lamps were few, by comparison with other inhabited worlds, and the ground-car needed lights of its own to guide its driver over a paved surface that needed repair. By those moving lights other depressing things could be seen. Untidiness.

Buildings not kept up to perfection. Evidences of apathy. The road hadn't been cleaned lately. There was litter here and there.

Even the fact that there were no stars added to the feeling of wretchedness and gloom and—ultimately—of hunger.

Maril spoke nervously to the driver.

"The famine isn't any better?"

He moved his head in negation, but did not speak.

"I left—two years ago," said Maril. "It was just beginning then. Rationing hadn't started then—"

The driver said evenly;

"There's rationing now!"

The car went on and on. A vast open space appeared ahead. Lights about its perimeter seemed few and pale.

"E-everything seems—worse. Even the lights."

"Using all the power," said the driver, "to warm up ground to grow crops where it ought to be winter. Not doing too well, either."

Calhoun knew, somehow, that Maril moistened her lips.

"I—was sent," she explained to the driver, "to go ashore on Trent and then make my way to Weald. I—mailed reports of what I found out back to Trent. Somebody got them back to here whenever—it was possible."

The driver said;

"Everybody knows the man on Trent disappeared. Maybe he got caught, maybe somebody saw him without makeup. Or maybe he just quit being one of us. What's the difference? No use!"

Calhoun found himself wincing a little. The driver was not angry. He was hopeless. But men should not despair. They shouldn't accept hostility from those about them as a device of fate for their destruction. They shouldn't...

Maril said quickly to him;

"You understand? Dara's a heavy-metals planet. There aren't many light elements in our soil. Potassium is scarce. So our ground isn't very fertile. Before the Plague we traded heavy metals and manufactures for imports of food and potash. But since the Plague we've had no off-planet commerce. We've been—quarantined."

"I gathered as much," said Calhoun. "It was up to Med Service to see that that didn't happen. It's up to Med Service now to see that it stops."

"Too late now for anything," said the driver, "whatever Med Service may be! They're talking about cutting down our population so there'll be food enough for some to live. There are two questions about it: who's to be kept alive and why."

The ground-car aimed now for a cluster of faintly brighter lights on the far side of the great open space. They enlarged as they grew nearer. Maril said hesitantly;

"There was someone—Korvan—" Calhoun didn't catch the rest of the name, Maril said hesitantly; "He was working on food-plants. I—thought he might accomplish something…"

The driver said caustically;

"Sure! Everybody's heard about him! He came up with a wonderful thing! He and his outfit worked out a way to process weeds so they can be eaten. And they can. You can fill your belly and not feel hungry, but it's like eating hay. You starve just the same. He's still working. Head of a government division."

The ground-car passed through a gate. It stopped before a lighted door. The armed men hanging to its outside dropped off. They watched Calhoun closely as he stepped out with Murgatroyd riding on his shoulder.

Minutes later they faced a hastily-summoned group of officials of the Darian government. For a ship to land on

Dara was so remarkable an event that it called practically for a cabinet meeting. And Calhoun noted that they were no better fed than the guards at the space-port.

They regarded Calhoun and Maril with oddly burning eyes. It was, of course, because the two of them showed no signs of hunger. They obviously had not been on short rations.

"My name is Calhoun," said Calhoun briskly. "I've the usual Med Service credentials. Now…"

He did not wait to be questioned. He told them of the appalling state of things in the Twelfth Sector of the Med Service, so that men had been borrowed from other sectors to remedy the intolerable, and he was one of them. He told of his arrival at Weald and what had happened there, from the excessively cautious insistence that he prove he was not a Darian, to the arrival of the death-ship from Orede. He was giving them the news affecting them, as they had not heard it before.

He went on to tell of his stop at Orede and his purpose, and his encounter with the men he found there. When he finished there was silence. He broke it.

"Now," he said, "Maril's an agent of yours. She can add to what I've told you. I'm Med Service. I have a job to do here to repair what wasn't done before. I should make a planetary health inspection and make recommendations for the improvement of the state of things. I'll be glad if you'll arrange for me to talk to your health officials. Things look bad, and something should be done."

Someone laughed without mirth.

"What will you recommend for long-continued undernourishment?" he asked derisively. "That's our health problem!"

"I recommend food," said Calhoun.

"Where'll you fill the prescription?"

"I've the answer to that, too," said Calhoun curtly. "I'll want to talk to any space-pilots you've got. Get your astrogators together and I think they'll approve my idea."

The silence was totally skeptical.

"Orede…"

"Not Orede," said Calhoun. "Weald will be hunting that planet over for Darians. If they find any, they'll drop bombs here."

"Our only space-pilots," said a tall man, presently, "are on Orede now. If you've told the truth, they'll probably head back because of your warning. They should bring meat."

His mouth worked peculiarly, and Calhoun knew that it was at the thought of food.

"Which," said another man sharply, "goes to the hospitals! I haven't tasted meat in two years!"

"Nobody has," growled another man still. "But here's this man Calhoun. I'm not convinced he can work magic, but we can find out if he lies. Put a guard on his ship. Otherwise let our health men give him his head. They'll find out if he's from this Medical Service he tells of! And this Maril—"

"I—can be identified," said Maril. "I was sent to gather information and sent it in secret writing to one of us on Trent. I have a family here. They'll know me! And I—there was someone who was working on foods, and I believe he—made it possible to use—all sorts of vegetation for food. He will identify me."

Someone laughed harshly.

"Oh, yes!" said a man with a blue forehead. "He's a valuable man! Within the year he's come up with a way to make his weeds taste like any food one chooses. If we decide to cut our population, we'll simply give the people to be eliminated all they want to eat of his products. They'll not be hungry. They'll be quite happy. But they'll die for lack of nourishment. He's volunteered to prove it painless by going through it himself!"

Maril swallowed.

"I'd like to see him," she repeated. "And my family."

Some of the blue-splotched men turned away. A broad-shouldered man said bluntly;

"Don't look for them to be glad to see you. And you'd better not show yourself in public. You've been well fed. You'll be hated for that."

Maril began to cry. Murgatroyd said bewilderedly;

"*Chee! Chee!*"

Calhoun held him close. There was confusion. And Calhoun found the Minister of Health at hand—he looked most harried of all the officials gathered to question Calhoun—and proposed that he get a look at the hospital situation right away.

It wasn't practical. With all the population on half rations or less, when night came people needed to sleep. Most people, indeed, slept as many hours out of the traditional twenty-four as they could manage. It was much more pleasant to sleep than to be awake and constantly nagged at by continued hunger. And there was the matter of simple decency. Continuous gnawing hunger had an embittering effect upon everyone. Quarrelsomeness was a common experience. And people who would normally be the leaders of opinion felt shame because they were obsessed by thoughts of food. It was best when people slept.

Still, Calhoun was in the hospitals by daybreak. What he found moved him to savage anger. There were too many sick children. In every case undernourishment contributed to their sickness. And there was not enough food to make them well. Doctors and nurses denied themselves food to spare it for their patients.

Calhoun brought out hormones and enzymes and medicaments from the Med Ship while the guard in the ship looked on. He demonstrated the processes of synthesis and autocatalysis that enabled such small samples to be multiplied indefinitely. He was annoyed by a clamorous appetite. There were some doctors who ignored the irony of medical techniques being taught to cure non-nutritional disease, when everybody was half-fed, or less. They approved of Calhoun. They even approved of Murgatroyd when Calhoun explained his function.

He was, of course, a Med Service *tormal*, and *tormals* were creatures of talent. They'd originally been found on a planet in the Deneb area, and they were engaging and friendly small animals, but the remarkable fact about them was that they couldn't contract any disease. Not any. They had a built-in, explosive reaction to bacterial and viral toxins, and there hadn't yet been any pathogenic organism discovered to which a *tormal* could not more or less immediately develop antibody-resistance. So that in interstellar medicine *tormals* were priceless. Let Murgatroyd be infected with however localized, however specialized an inimical organism, and presently some highly valuable defensive substance could be isolated from his blood and he'd remain in his usual exuberant good health. When the antibody was analyzed by those techniques of microanalysis the Service had developed,—why—that was that. The antibody could be synthesized and one could attack any epidemic with confidence.

The tragedy for Dara was, of course, that no Med Ship had come there, three generations ago, when the Dara plague raged. Worse, after the plague Weald was able to exert pressure which only a criminally incompetent Med Service director would have permitted. But criminal incompetence and its consequences was what Calhoun had been loaned to Sector Twelve to help remedy.

He was not at ease, though. No ship arrived from Orede to bear out his account of an attempt to get that lonely world evacuated before Weald discovered it had blueskins on it. Maril had vanished, to visit or return to her family, or perhaps to consult with the mysterious Korvan who'd arranged for her to leave Dara to be a spy, and had advised her simply to make a new life somewhere else, abandoning a famine-ridden, despised, and outcast world. Calhoun had learned of two achievements the same Korvan had made for his world. Neither was remarkably constructive. He'd offered to prove the value of the second by dying of it. Which might make him a very admirable character, or he could have a passion for martyrdom,—which is much more common than most people think. In two days Calhoun was irritable enough from unaccustomed hunger to suspect the worst of him.

And there was Weald to worry about. Weald was hysterically resolved to end what it considered the blueskin menace for once and for all. There were parallels to such unreasoning frenzy even in the ancient history of Earth. A word still remained in the dictionaries referring to it. Genocide.

Meanwhile Calhoun worked doggedly; in the hospitals while the patients were awake and in the Med Ship—under guard—afterward. He had hunger cramps now, but he tested a plastic cube with a thriving biological culture in it. He worked at increasing his store of it. He'd snipped samples of pigmented skin from dead patients in the hospitals, and examined the pigmented areas, and very, very painstakingly verified a theory. It took an electron microscope to do it, but he found a virus in the blue patches which matched the type discovered on Tralee. The Tralee viruses had effects which were passed on from mother to child, and heredity had been charged with the observed results of quasi-living viral particles. And then Calhoun very, very carefully introduced into a virus culture the material he had been growing in a plastic cube. He watched what happened.

He was satisfied, so much so that immediately afterward he barely managed to stagger off to bed.

That night the ship from Orede came in, packed with frozen bloody carcasses of cattle. Calhoun knew nothing of it. But next morning Maril came back. There were shadows under her eyes and her expression was of someone who has lost everything that had meaning in her life.

"I'm all right," she insisted, when Calhoun commented. "I've been visiting my family. I've seen—Korvan. I'm quite all right."

"You haven't eaten any better than I have," Calhoun observed.

"I—couldn't!" admitted Maril. "My sisters—my little sisters—so thin... There's rationing for everybody and it's all efficiently arranged. They even had rations for me. But I couldn't eat! I—gave most of my food to my sisters and they—squabbled over it!"

Calhoun said nothing. There was nothing to say. Then she said in a no less desolate tone;

"Korvan said I was foolish to come back."

"He could be right," said Calhoun.

"But I had to!" protested Maril. "Because I—I've been eating all I wanted to, on Weald and in the ship, and I'm ashamed because they're half-starved and I'm not. And when you see what hunger does to them... It's terrible to be half-starved and not able to think of anything but food!"

"I hope," said Calhoun, "to do something about that. If I can get hold of an astrogator or two."

"The—ship that was on Orede came in during the night," Maril told him shakily. "It was loaded with frozen meat, but one ship-load's not enough to make a difference on a whole planet! And if Weald hunts for us on Orede, we daren't go back for more meat."

She said abruptly;

"There are some prisoners. They were miners. They were crowded out of the ship. The Darians who'd stampeded the cattle took them prisoners. They had to!"

"True," said Calhoun. "It wouldn't have been wise to leave Wealdians around on Orede with their throats cut. Or living, either, to tell about a rumor of blueskins. Even if their throats will be cut now. Is that the program?"

Maril shivered.

"No... They'll be put on short rations like everybody else. And people will watch them. The Wealdians expect to die of plague any minute because they've been with Darians. So people look at them and laugh. But it's not funny."

"It's natural," said Calhoun, "but perhaps lacking in charity. Look here! How about those astrogators? I need them for a job I have in mind."

Maril wrung her hands.

"C—come here," she said in a low tone.

There was an armed guard in the control-room of the ship. He'd watched Calhoun a good part of the previous day as Calhoun performed his mysterious work. He'd been off-duty and now was on duty again. He was bored. So long as Calhoun did not touch the control-board, though, he was uninterested. He didn't even turn his head when Maril led the way into the other cabin and slid the door shut.

"The astrogators are coming," she said swiftly. "They'll bring some boxes with them. They'll ask you to instruct them so they can handle our ship better. They lost themselves coming back from Orede, no, they didn't lose themselves, but they lost time—enough time almost to make an extra trip for meat. They need to be experts. I'm to come along, so they can be sure that what you teach them is what you've been doing right along."

Calhoun said;

"Well?"

"They're crazy!" said Maril vehemently. "They knew Weald would do something monstrous sooner or later. But they're going to try to stop it by more monstrousness sooner! Not everybody agrees, but there are enough. So they want to use your ship—it's faster in overdrive and so on. And they'll go to Weald—in this ship—and—they say they'll give Weald something to keep it busy without bothering us!"

Calhoun said drily;

"This pays me off for being too sympathetic with blueskins! But if I'd been hungry for a couple of years, and was despised to boot by the people who kept me hungry, I suppose I might react the same way. No," he said curtly as she opened her lips to speak again. "Don't tell me the trick. Considering everything, there's only one trick it could be. But I doubt profoundly that it would work. All right."

He slid the door back and returned to the control-room. Maril followed him. He said detachedly;

"I've been working on a problem outside of the food one. It isn't the time to talk about it right now, but I think I've solved it."

Maril turned her head, listening. There were footsteps on the tarmac outside the ship. Both doors of the airlock were open. Four men came in. They were young men who did not look quite as hungry as most Darians, but there was a reason for that. Their leader introduced himself and the others. They were the astrogators of the ship Dara had built to try to bring food from Orede. They were not good enough, said their self-appointed leader. They overshot their destination. They came out of overdrive too far off line. They needed instructions.

Calhoun nodded, and observed that he'd been asking for them.

"We've got orders," said their leader, steadily, "to come on board and learn from you how to handle this ship. It's better than the one we've got."

"I asked for you," repeated Calhoun. "I've an idea I'll explain as we go along. Those boxes?"

Someone was passing in iron boxes through the airlock. One of the four very carefully brought them inside.

"They're rations," said a second young man. "We don't go anywhere without rations—except Orede."

"Orede, yes. I think we were shooting at each other there," said Calhoun pleasantly. "Weren't we?"

"Yes," said the young man.

He was neither cordial nor antagonistic. He was impassive. Calhoun shrugged.

"Then we can take off immediately. Here's the communicator and there's the button. You might call the grid and arrange for us to be lifted."

The young man seated himself at the control-board. Very professionally, he went through the routine of preparing to lift by landing-grid, which routine has not changed in two hundred years. He went briskly ahead until the order to lift. Then Calhoun stopped him.

"Hold it!"

He pointed to the airlock. Both doors were open. The young man at the control-board flushed vividly. One of the others closed and dogged the doors.

The ship lifted. Calhoun watched with seeming negligence. But he found occasion for a dozen corrections of procedure. This was presumably a training voyage of his own suggestion. Therefore when the blueskin pilot would have flung the Med Ship into undirected overdrive, Calhoun grew stern. He insisted on a destination. He suggested Weald.

The young men glanced at each other and accepted the suggestion. He made the acting pilot look up the intrinsic business of its sun and measure its apparent brightness from just off Dara. He made him estimate the change in brightness to be expected after so many hours in overdrive, if one broke out to measure.

The first blueskin student pilot ended a Calhoun-determined tour of duty with rather more of respect for Calhoun than he'd had at the beginning. The second was anxious to show up better than the first. Calhoun drilled him in the use of brightness-charts, by which the changes in apparent brightness of stars between overdrive hops could be correlated with angular changes to give a three-dimensional picture of the nearer heavens. It was a highly necessary art which had not been worked out on Dara, and the prospective astrogators became absorbed in this and other fine points of space-piloting. They'd done enough, in a few trips to Orede, to realize that they needed to know more. Calhoun showed them.

Calhoun did not try to make things easy for them. He was hungry and easily annoyed. It was sound training tactics to be severe, and to phrase all suggestions as commands. He put the four young men in command of the ship in turn, under his direction. He continued to use Weald as a destination, but he set up problems in which the Med Ship came out of overdrive pointing in an unknown direction and with a precessory motion. He made the third of his students identify Weald in the celestial globe containing hundreds of millions of stars, and get on course in overdrive toward it. The fourth was suddenly required to compute the distance to Weald from such data as he could get from observation, without reference to any records.

By this time the first man was chafing to take a second turn. Calhoun gave each of them a second gruelling lesson.

He gave them, in fact, a highly condensed but very sound course in the art of travel in space. His young students took command in four-hour watches, with at least one breakout from overdrive in each watch. He built up enthusiasm in them. They ignored the discomfort of being hungry, though there had been no reason for them to stint on food in Orede—in growing pride in what they came to know.

When Weald was a first-magnitude star, the four were not highly qualified astrogators, to be sure, but they were vastly better spacemen than at the beginning. Inevitably, their attitude toward Calhoun was respectful. He'd been irritable and right. To the young, the combination is impressive.

Maril had served as passenger only. In theory she was to compare Calhoun's lessons with his practise when alone. But he did nothing on this journey which—teaching considered— was different from the two interstellar journeys Maril had made with him. She occupied the sleeping-cabin during two of the six watches of each ship-day. She operated the food-readier, which was almost completely emptied of its original store of food;—confiscated by the government of Dara. That amount of food would make no difference to the planet, but it was wise for everyone on Dara to be equally ill-fed.

On the sixth day out from Dara, the sun of Weald had a magnitude of minus five-tenths. The electron telescope could detect its larger planets, especially a gas-giant fifth-orbit world of high albedo. Calhoun had his four students estimate its distance again, pointing out the difference that could be made in breakout position if the Med Ship were mis-aimed by as much as one second of arc.

"That does it," Calhoun announced cheerfully. "That's the last order I'll give you. You're graduate pilots from here on! Relax and have some coffee."

"And now," said Calhoun, "I suppose you'll tell me the truth about those boxes you brought on board. You said they were rations, but they haven't been opened in six days. I have an idea what they mean, but you tell me."

The four looked uncomfortable. There was a long pause.

"They could be," said Calhoun detachedly, "cultures to be dumped on Weald. Weald is making plans to wipe out Dara. So some fool has decided to get Weald too busy fighting a plague of its own to bother with you. Is that right?"

The young men stirred uneasily. "Well—l—l, sir," said one of them, unhappily, "that's what we were ordered to do."

"I object," said Calhoun. "It wouldn't work. I just left Weald a little while back, remember. They've been telling themselves that some day Dara would try that. They've made preparations to fight any imaginable contagion you could drop on them. Every so often somebody claims it's happening. It wouldn't work."

"But—"

"In fact," said Calhoun, "I will not permit you to do anything of the kind."

One of the young men, staring at Calhoun, nodded suddenly. His eyes closed. He jerked his head erect and looked bewildered. A second sank heavily into a chair. He said remotely, "Thish sfunny!" and abruptly went to sleep. The third found his knees giving away. He paid elaborate attention to them, stiffening them. But they yielded like rubber and he went slowly down to the floor. The fourth said thickly with difficulty, yet reproachfully;

"'Thought y'were our frien'!"

He collapsed.

Calhoun very soberly tied them hand and foot and laid them out comfortably on the floor. Maril watched, white-faced, her hand to her throat. "What have you done to them? Are they dead?"

"No," said Calhoun, "just drugged. They'll wake up presently."

Maril said in a tense and desperate whisper;

"You're—betraying us! You're going to take us to Weald."

"No," said Calhoun. "We'll only orbit around it. First, though, I want to get rid of those damned packed-up cultures. They're dead, by the way. I killed them with supersonics a couple of days ago, while a fine argument was going on about distance-measurements by variable Cepheids of known period."

He put the four boxes carefully in the waste-disposal unit. He operated it. The boxes and their contents streamed out to space in the form of metallic and other vapors. Calhoun sat at the control-desk.

"I'm a Med Service man," he said detachedly. "I couldn't cooperate in the spread of plague, anyhow, though a useful epidemic might be another matter. But the important thing right now is not keeping Weald busy with troubles to increase their hatred of Dara. It's getting some food for Dara. And driblets won't help. What's needed is in thousands of tons,— or tens of thousands." Then he said; "Overdrive coming, Murgatroyd! Hold fast!"

The universe vanished. The customary unpleasant sensations accompanied the change. Murgatroyd burped.

Earth's sun, from Earth, is of magnitude roughly minus thirty-six.

CHAPTER SIX

A large part of the firmament was blotted out by the blindingly bright half-disk of Weald, as it shone in the sunshine. It had ice-caps at its poles, and there were seas, and the mottled look of land which had that carefully maintained balance of woodland and cultivated areas which so effective in climate control. The Med Ship floated free, and

Calhoun fretfully monitored all the beacon frequencies known to man.

There was relative silence inside the ship. Maril watched Calhoun in a sort of despairing indecision. The four young blueskins still slept, still bound hand and foot upon the control-room floor. Murgatroyd regarded them, and Maril, and Calhoun in turn, and his small and furry forehead wrinkled helplessly.

"They can't have landed what I'm looking for!" protested Calhoun as his search had no result. "They can't. It would be too sensible for them to have done it!"

Murgatroyd said "*Chee!*" in a subdued voice.

"But where the devil did they put them?" demanded Calhoun. "A polar orbit would be ridiculous! They—" Then he grunted in disgust. "Oh! Of course! Now, where's the landing-grid?"

He worked busily for minutes, checking the position of the Wealdian landing-grid—mapped in the Sector Directory—against the look of continents and seas on the half-disk so plainly visible outside. He found what he wanted. He put on the ship's solar-system drive.

"I wish," he complained to Maril, "I wish I could think straight the first time! And it's so obvious! If you want to put something out in space, and not have it interfere with traffic, in what sort of orbit and at what distance will you put it?"

Maril did not answer.

"Obviously," said Calhoun, "you'll put it as far as possible from the landing-pattern of ships coming in to the space-port. You'll put it on the opposite side of the planet. And you'll want it to stay out of the way, where anybody can know it is at any time of the day or night without having to calculate anything. So you'll put it out in orbit so it will revolve around Weald in exactly one day, neither more or less, and you'll put it above the equator. And then it will remain quite stationary above one spot on the planet, a hundred and eighty degrees longitude away from the landing-grid and directly over the equator."

He scribbled for a moment.

"Which means forty-two thousand miles high, give or take a few hundred, and—here! And I was hunting for it in a close-in orbit!"

He grumbled to himself. He waited while the solar-system drive pushed the Med Ship a quarter of the way around the bright planet below. The sunset line vanished and the planet's disk became a complete circle. Then Calhoun listened to the monitor earphones again, and grunted once more, and changed course, and presently made a noise indicating satisfaction.

Again presently he abandoned instrument-control and peered directly out of a port, handling the solar-system drive with great care. Murgatroyd said depressedly;

"*Chee!*"

"Stop worrying," commanded Calhoun. "We haven't been challenged, and there is a beacon transmitter at work, just to make sure that nobody bumps into what we're looking for. It's a great help, because we do want to bump,—gently."

Stars swung across the port out of which he looked. Something dark appeared,—and then straight lines and exact curvings. Even Maril, despairing and bewildered as she was, caught sight of something vastly larger than the Med Ship, floating in space. She stared. The Med Ship maneuvered very cautiously. She saw another large object. A third. A fourth. There seemed to be dozens of them.

They were space-ships, huge by comparison with Aesclipus Twenty. They floated as the Med Ship did. They did not drive. They were not in formation. They were not at even distances from each other. They did not point in the same direction. They swung in emptiness like derelicts.

Calhoun jockeyed his small ship with infinite care. Presently there came the gentlest of impacts and then a clanking sound. The appearance out the vision-port became stationary, but still unbelievable. The Med Ship was grappled magnetically to a vast surface of welded metal.

Calhoun relaxed. He opened a wall-panel and brought out a vacuum suit. He began briskly to get it on.

"Things move smoothly," he commented. "We weren't challenged. So it's extremely unlikely that we were spotted. Our friends on the floor ought to begin to come to shortly. And I'm going to find out now whether I'm a hero or in sure-enough trouble!"

Maril said drearily;

"I don't know what you've done, except—"

Calhoun blinked at her, in the act of hauling the vacuum suit over his shoulders.

"Isn't it self-evident?" he demanded. "I've been giving astrogation lessons to these characters. I certainly didn't do it to help them dump germ-cultures on Weald! I brought them here! Don't you see the point? These are space-ships. They're in orbit around Weald. They're not manned and they're not controlled. In fact, they're nothing but sky-riding storage bins!"

He seemed to consider the explanation complete. He wriggled his arms into the sleeves and gloves of the suit. He slung the air-tanks over his shoulder and hooked them to the suit.

"I'll be back," he said. "I hope with good news. I've reason to be hopeful, though, because these Wealdians are very practical men. They have things all prepared and tidy. I suspect I'll find these ships with stores of air and fuel—maybe even food—so that if Weald should manage to make a deal for the stuff stored out here in them, they'd only have to bring out crews."

He lifted the space-helmet down from its rack and put it on. He tested it, reading the tank air-pressure, power-storage, and other data from the lighted miniature instruments visible through pinholes above his eye-level. He fastened a space-rope about himself, speaking through the helmet's opened face-plate.

"If our friends should wake up before I get back," he added, "please restrain them. I'd hate to be marooned."

He went waddling into the airlock with the coil of space-rope over one vacuum-suited arm. The inner lock door closed behind him A little later Maril heard the outer lock open. Then soundlessness.

Murgatroyd whimpered a little. Maril shivered. Calhoun had gone out of the ship to nothingness. He'd said that what he was looking for—and what he'd found—was forty-two thousand miles from Weald. One could imagine falling forty-two thousand miles, where one couldn't imagine falling a light-year. Calhoun was walking on the steel plates of a gigantic space-ship which floated among dozens of its fellows, all seeming derelicts and seemingly abandoned. He was able to walk on the nearest because of magnetic-soled shoes. He trusted his life to them and to a flimsy space-rope which trailed after him out the Med Ship's airlock.

Time passed. A clock ticked in that hurried tempo of five ticks to the second which has been the habit of clocks since time immemorial. Very small and trivial noises came from the background tape, preventing utter silence from hanging intolerably in the ship. They were traffic-sounds, recorded on a world no one knew how many light-years distant, and nobody knew when. There were sounds as of voices, too faint to suggest words, but imparting a feel of life and activity to a soundless ship.

Maril found herself listening tensely for something else. One of the four bound blueskins snored, and stirred, and slept again. Murgatroyd gazed about unhappily, and swung down to the control-room floor, and then paused for lack of any place to go or thing to do. He sat down and began half-heartedly to lick his whiskers. Maril stirred.

Murgatroyd looked at her hopefully.

"*Chee?*" he asked shrilly.

She shook her head. It became a habit to act as if Murgatroyd were a human being.

"N-no," she said unsteadily. "Not yet."

More time passed. An unbearably long time. Then there was the faintest of clankings. It repeated. Then, abruptly, there were noises in the airlock. They continued. They were fumbling noises.

The outer airlock door closed. The inner door opened. Dense white fog came out of it. There was motion. Calhoun followed the fog out of the lock. He carried objects which had been weightless, but were suddenly heavy in the ship's gravity-field. There were two space-suits and a curious assortment of parcels. He spread them out, flipped aside the face-plate, and said briskly;

"This stuff is cold! Turn a heater on it, will you Maril?"

He began to work his way out of his vacuum-suit.

"Item," he said. "The ships are fuelled *and* provisioned. A practical tribe, the Wealdians! The ships are ready to take off as soon as they're warmed up inside. A half-degree sun doesn't radiate heat enough to keep a ship warm, when the rest of the cosmos is effectively near zero Kelvin. Here, point the heaters like this."

He adjusted the radiant-heat dispensers. The fog disappeared where their beams played. But the metal space-suits glistened and steamed,—and the steam disappeared within inches. They were so completely and utterly cold that they condensed the air about them as a liquid, which reëvaporated to make fog, which warmed up and disappeared and was immediately replaced.

"Item," said Calhoun again, getting his arms out of the vacuum-suit sleeves. "The controls are pretty nearly standard. Our sleeping friends will be able to astrogate them back to Dara without trouble, provided only that nobody comes out here to bother us before they leave."

He shed the last of the space-suit, stepping out of its legs.

"And," he finished wrily, "I brought back an emergency supply of ship-provisions for everybody concerned, but find that I'm idiot enough to feel that they'll choke me if I eat them while Dara's still starving."

Maril said;

"But—there isn't any hope for Dara! No real hope!"

He gaped at her.

"What do you think we're here for?"

He set to work to restore his four recent students to consciousness. It was not a difficult task. The dosage, mixed in the coffee he had given them earlier, was a light one. Calhoun took the precaution of disarming them first, but presently four hot-eyed young men glared at him.

"I'm calling," said Calhoun, holding a blaster negligently in his hand, "I'm calling for volunteers. There's a famine on Dara. There've been unmanageable crop-surpluses on Weald. On Dara, the government grimly rations every ounce of food. On Weald, the government has been buying up surplus grain to keep the price up. To save storage costs, it's loaded the grain into out-of-date space-ships it once used to stand sentry over Dara to keep it out of space when there was another famine there. Those ships have been put out in orbit, where we're hooked on to one of them. It's loaded with half a million bushels of grain. I've brought space-suits from it, I've turned on the heaters in its interior, and I've set its overdrive unit for a hop to Dara. Now I'm calling for volunteers to take half a million bushels of grain to where it's needed. Do I get any volunteers?"

He got four. Not immediately, because they were ashamed that he'd made it impossible to carry out their original fanatic plan, and now offered something much better to make up for it. They raged. But half a million bushels of grain meant that people who must otherwise die might live.

Ultimately, truculently, first one and then another angrily agreed.

"Good!" said Calhoun. "Now, how many of you dare risk the trip alone? I've got one grain-ship warming up. There are plenty of others around us. Every one of you can take a ship and half a million bushels to Dara, if you have the nerve?"

The atmosphere changed. Suddenly they clamored for the task he offered them. They were still acutely uncomfortable. He'd bossed them and taught them until they felt capable and glamorous and proud. Then he'd pinned their ears back. But if they returned to Dara with four enemy ships and unimaginable quantities of food with which to break the famine…

There was work to be done first, of course. Only one ship was so far warming up. Three more had to be entered, in space-suits, and each had to have its interior warmed so breathable air could exist inside it, and at least part of the stored provisions had to be brought up to reasonable temperature for use on the journey. Then the overdrive unit had to be inspected and set for the length of journey that a direct overdrive hop to Dara would mean, and Calhoun had to make sure again that each of the four could identify Dara's sun under all circumstances and aim for it with the requisite high precision, both before going into overdrive and after breakout. When all that was accomplished, Calhoun might reasonably hope that they'd arrive. But it wasn't a certainty.

Still, presently his four students shook hands with him, with the fine tolerance of young men intending much greater achievements than their teacher. They wouldn't speak on communicator again, because their messages might be picked up on Weald.

Of course for this action to be successful, it had to be performed with the stealth of sneak-thieves.

What seemed a long time passed. Then one ship turned slowly upon some unseen axis. It wavered back and forth, seeking a point of aim. A second twisted in its place. A third put on the barest trace of solar-system drive to get clear of the rest. The fourth...

One ship vanished. It had gone into overdrive, heading for Dara at many times the speed of light. Another. Two more.

That was all. The remainder of the fleet hung clumsily in emptiness. And Calhoun worriedly went over in his mind the lessons he'd given in such a pathetically small number of days. If the four ships reached Dara, their pilots would be heroes. Calhoun had presented them with that estate over their bitter objection. But they would glory in it, if they reached Dara.

Maril looked at him with very strange eyes.

"Now what?" she asked.

"We hang around," said Calhoun, "to see if anybody comes up from Weald to find out what's happened. It's always possible to pick up a sort of signal when a ship goes into overdrive. Usually it doesn't mean a thing. Nobody pays any attention. But if somebody comes out here—"

"What?"

"It'll be regrettable," said Calhoun. He was suddenly very tired. "It'll spoil any chance of our coming back and stealing some more food—like interstellar mice. If they find out what we've done they'll expect us to try it again. They might get set to fight. Or they might simply land the rest of these ships."

"If I'd realized what you were about," said Maril, "I'd have joined in the lessons. I could have piloted a ship."

"You wouldn't have wanted to," said Calhoun. He yawned. "You wouldn't want to be a heroine."

"Why?"

"Korvan," said Calhoun. He yawned again. "I've asked about him. He's been trying very desperately to deserve well of his fellow blueskins. All he's accomplished is develop a way to starve painlessly. He wouldn't feel comfortable with a girl who'd helped make starving unnecessary. He'd admire you politely, but he'd never marry you. And you know it."

She shook her head, but it was not easy to tell whether she denied the reaction of Korvan—whom Calhoun had never met—or denied that he was more important to her than anything else. The last was what Calhoun plainly implied.

"You don't seem to be trying to be a hero!" she protested.

"I'd enjoy it," admitted Calhoun, "but I have a job to do. It's got to be done. It's much more important than being admired."

"You could take another ship back," she told him. "It would be worth more to Dara than the Med Ship is! And then everybody would realize that you'd planned everything."

"Ah!" said Calhoun. "But you've no idea how much this ship matters to Dara!"

He seated himself at the controls. He slipped headphones over his ears. He listened. Very, very carefully, he monitored all the wave-lengths and wave-forms he could discover in use on Weald. There was no mention of the oddity of behavior of shiploads of surplus grain aloft. There was no mention of the ships at all. But there was plenty of mention of Dara, and blueskins, and of the vicious political fight now going on to see which political party could promise the most complete protection against blueskins.

After a full hour of it, Calhoun flipped off his receptor and swung the Med Ship to an exact, painstakingly precise aim at the sun around which Dara rolled. He said;

"Overdrive coming, Murgatroyd!"

Murgatroyd grabbed. The stars went out and the universe reeled and the Med Ship became a sort of cosmos all its own.

Calhoun yawned again.

"Now there's nothing to be done for a day or two," he said wearily, "and I'm beginning to understand why people sleep all they can, on Dara. It's one way not to feel hungry."

Maril said tensely;

"You're going back? After they took the ship from you?"

"The job's not finished," he explained. "Not even the famine's ended, and the famine's a second-order effect. If there were no such thing as a blueskin, there'd be no famine. Food could be traded for. We've got to do something to make sure there are no more famines."

She looked at him oddly.

"It would be desirable," she said with irony. "But you can't do it."

"Not today, no," he admitted. Then he said longingly, "I'm about to catch up on some sleep."

Maril rose and went into the other cabin. He settled down into the chair and fell instantly asleep.

For very many ship-hours, then, there was no action or activity or happening of any imaginable consequence in the Med Ship. Very, very far away, light-years distant and light years apart, four shiploads of grain hurtled toward the famine-stricken planet of blueskins. Each great ship had a single semi-skilled blueskin for pilot and crew. Thousands of millions of suns blazed with violence appropriate to their stellar types in a galaxy of which a very small proportion had been explored and colonized by humanity. The human race was now to be counted in quadrillions on scores of hundreds of inhabited worlds, but the tiny Med Ship seemed the least significant of all possible created things. It could travel between star-systems and even star-clusters, but it was not yet capable of crossing the continent of suns on which the human race arose. And between any two solar systems the journeying of the Med Ship consumed much time. Which would be maddening for someone with no work to do or no resources in himself, or herself.

On the second ship-day Calhoun labored painstakingly and somewhat distastefully at the little biological laboratory. Maril watched him in a sort of brooding silence. Murgatroyd slept much of the time, with his furry tail wrapped meticulously across his nose.

Toward the end of the day Calhoun finished his task. He had a matter of six or seven cubic centimeters of clear liquid as the conclusion of a long process of culturing, and examination by microscope, and again culturing plus final filtration. He looked at a clock and calculated time.

"Better wait until tomorrow," he observed, and put the bit of clear liquid in a temperature-controlled place of safe-keeping.

"What is it?" asked Maril. "What's it for?"

"It's part of a job I have on hand," said Calhoun. He considered. "How about some music?"

She looked astonished. But he set up an instrument and fed microtape into it and settled back to listen. Then there was music such as she had never heard before. Again it was a device to counteract isolation and monotonous between-planet voyages. To keep it from losing its effectiveness, Calhoun rationed himself on music, as on other things. Calhoun deliberately went for weeks between uses of his recordings, so that music was an event to be looked forward to and cherished.

When he tapered off the stirring symphonies of Kun Gee with tranquilizing, soothing melodies from the Rim School of composers, Maril regarded him with a very peculiar gaze indeed.

"I think I understand now," she said slowly, "why you don't act like other people. Toward me, for example. The way you live gives you what other people have to try to get in crazy ways,—making their work feed their vanity, and justify pride, and make them feel significant. But you can put your whole mind on your work."

He thought it over.

"Med Ship routine is designed to keep one healthy in his mind," he admitted. "It works pretty well. It satisfies all my mental appetites. But naturally there are instincts—"

She waited. He did not finish.

"What do you do about instincts that work and music and such things can't satisfy?"

Calhoun grinned wrily;

"I'm stern with them. I have to be."

He stood up and plainly expected her to go into the other cabin for the night. She did.

It was after breakfast-time of the next ship-day when he got out the sample of clear liquid he'd worked so long to produce. "We'll see how it works," he observed. "Murgatroyd's handy in case of a slip-up. It's perfectly safe so long as he's aboard and there are only the two of us."

She watched as he injected half a cc under his own skin. Then she shivered a little.

"What will it do?"

"That remains to be seen." He paused a moment. "You and I," he said with some dryness, "make a perfect test for anything. If you catch something from me, it will be infective indeed!"

She gazed at him utterly without comprehension.

He took his own temperature. He brought out the folios which were his orders, covering each of the planets he should give a standard Medical Service inspection. Weald was there. Dara wasn't. But a Med Service man has much freedom of action, even when only keeping up the routine of normal Med Service. When catching up on badly neglected operations, he necessarily has much more. Calhoun went over the folios.

Two hours later he took his temperature again. He looked pleased. He made an entry in the ship's log. Two hours later yet he found himself drinking thirstily and looked more pleased still. He made another entry in the log and matter-of-factly drew a small quantity of blood from his own vein and called to Murgatroyd. Murgatroyd submitted amiably to the very trivial operation Calhoun carried out. Calhoun put away the equipment and saw Maril staring at him with a certain look of shock.

"It doesn't hurt him," Calhoun explained. "Right after he's born there's a tiny spot on his flank that has the pain-nerves desensitized. Murgatroyd's all right. That's what he's for!"

"But he's—your friend!"

"He's my assistant. I don't ask anything of him that I can do myself. But we're both Med Service. And I do things for him that he can't do for himself. For example, I make coffee for him."

Murgatroyd heard the familiar word. He said;

"*Chee!*"

"Very well," agreed Calhoun. "We'll all have some."

He made coffee. Murgatroyd sipped at the cup especially made for his little paws. Once he scratched at the place on his flank which had no pain-nerves. It itched. But he was perfectly content. Murgatroyd would always be contented when he was somewhere near Calhoun.

Another hour went by. Murgatroyd climbed up into Calhoun's lap and with a determined air went to sleep there. Calhoun disturbed him long enough to get an instrument out of his pocket. He listened to Murgatroyd's heartbeat with it while Murgatroyd dozed.

"Maril," he said. "Write down something for me. The time, and ninety-six, and one-twenty over ninety-four."

She obeyed, not comprehending. Half an hour later—still not stirring to disturb Murgatroyd—he had her write down another time and sequence of figures, only slightly different from the first. Half an hour later still, a third set. But then he put Murgatroyd down, well satisfied.

He took his own temperature. He nodded.

"Murgatroyd and I have one more chore to do," he told her. "Would you go in the other cabin for a moment?"

She went disturbedly into the other cabin. Calhoun drew a sample of blood from the insensitive area on Murgatroyd's flank. Murgatroyd submitted with complete confidence in the man. In ten minutes Calhoun had diluted the sample, added an anticoagulant, shaken it up thoroughly, and filtered it to clarity with all red and white corpuscles removed. Another Med Ship man would have considered that Calhoun had had Murgatroyd prepare a splendid small sample of antibody-containing serum, in case something got out of hand. It would assuredly take care of two patients.

But a Med Ship man would also have known that it was simply one of those scrupulous precautions a Med Ship man takes when using cultures from store.

Calhoun put the sample away and called Maril back and offered no explanation. She said;

"I'll fix lunch." She hesitated. "You brought some food from the first Weald ship. Do you want it?"

He shook his head.

"I'm squeamish," he admitted. "The trouble on Dara is Med Service fault. Before my time, but still—I'll stick to rations until everybody eats."

He watched her unobtrusively as the day went on. Presently he considered that she was slightly flushed. Shortly after the evening meal of singularly unappetizing Darian rations, she drank thirstily. He did not comment. He brought out cards and showed her a complicated game of solitaire in which mental arithmetic and expert use of probability increased one's chance of winning.

By midnight, ship-time, she'd learned the game and played it absorbedly. Calhoun was able to scrutinize her without appearing to do so, and he was satisfied again. When he mentioned that the Med Ship should arrive off Dara in eight hours more, she put the cards away and went into the other cabin.

Calhoun wrote up the log. He added the notes that Maril had made for him, of Murgatroyd's pulse and blood-pressure after the injection of the same culture that produced fever and thirstiness in himself and later—without contact with him or the culture—in Maril. He put a professional comment at the end.

"The culture seems to have retained its normal characteristics during long storage in the spore state. It revived and reproduced rapidly. I injected .5 cc under my skin and in less than one hour my temperature was 30.8°C. An hour later it was 30.9°C. This was its peak. It immediately returned to normal. The only other observable symptom was slightly increased thirst. Blood-pressure and pulse remained normal. The other person in the Med Ship displayed the same symptoms, in prompt and complete repetition, without physical contact."

He went to sleep, with Murgatroyd curled up in his cubbyhole.

The Med Ship broke out of overdrive at 1300 hours, ship time. Calhoun made contact with the grid and was promptly lowered to the ground.

It was almost two hours later—1500 hours ship-time—when the people of Dara were informed by broadcast that Calhoun was publicly to be executed; immediately.

CHAPTER SEVEN

From the viewpoint of Darians, the decision of Calhoun's guilt and the decision to execute him were reasonable enough. Maril protested fiercely, and her testimony agreed with Calhoun's in every respect, but from a blueskin viewpoint their own statements were damning.

Calhoun had taken four young astrogators to space. They were the only semi-skilled space-pilots Dara had. There were no fully qualified men. Calhoun had asked for them, and taken them out to emptiness, and there he had instructed them in modern guidance-methods for ships of space. So far there was no disagreement. He'd proposed to make them more competent pilots; more capable of driving a ship to Orede, for example, to raid the enormous cattle-herds there. And he'd had them drive the Med Ship to Weald, against which there could be no objection.

But just before arrival he had tricked all four of them by giving them drugged coffee. He'd destroyed the lethal bacterial cultures they'd been ordered to dump on Weald. Then he'd sent the four student pilots off separately—so he and Maril claimed—in huge ships crammed with grain. But those ships were not to be believed in, anyhow. Nobody on

Dara could imagine stores of food bought up and stored away because it was useless; to keep up prices. Nobody believed in shiploads of grain to be had for the taking. They did know that the only four partially experienced space-pilots on Dara had been taken away and by Calhoun's own story sent out of the ship after they'd been drugged. Had they been trained, and had they been helped or even permitted to sow the seeds of plague on Weald, and had they come back prepared to pass on training to other men to handle other space-ships now feverishly being built in hidden places on Dara,—why—then Dara might have a chance of survival. But a space-battle with only partly trained pilots would be hazardous at best. With no trained pilots at all, it would be hopeless. So Calhoun, by his own story, appeared to have doomed every living being on Dara to massacre from the bombs of Weald.

It was this last angle which destroyed any chance of anybody believing in such fairy-tale objects as ships loaded down with grain. Calhoun had shattered Dara's feeble hope of resistance. Weald had some ships and could build or buy others faster than Dara could hope to construct them. Equally important, Weald had a plenitude of experienced spacemen to man some ships fully and train the crews of others. If it had become desperately busy fighting plague, then a fleet to exterminate life on Dara would be delayed. Dara might have gained time at least to build ships which could ram their enemies and destroy them that way.

But Calhoun had made it impossible. If he told the truth and Weald already had a fleet of huge ships which only needed to be emptied of grain and filled with guns and men—why—Dara was doomed. But if he did not tell the truth it was equally doomed by his actions. So Calhoun would be killed.

His execution was to take place in the open space of the landing-grid, with vision-cameras transmitting the sight over all the blueskin planet. Half-starved men, with grisly blue blotches on their skins, marched him to the center of the largest level space on the planet which was not desperately being cultivated. Their hatred showed in their expressions. Bitterness and fury surrounded Calhoun like a wall. Most of Dara would have liked to see him killed in a manner as atrocious as his crime, but no conceivable death would be satisfying.

So the affair was coldly businesslike, with not even insults offered to him. He was left to stand alone in the very center of the landing-grid floor. There were a hundred blasters which would fire upon him at the same instant. He would not only be killed; he would be destroyed. He would be vaporized by the blue-white flames poured upon him.

His death was remarkably close. Nothing remained but the order to fire, when loudspeakers from the landing-grid office froze everything. One of the grain-ships from Weald had broken out of overdrive and its pilot was triumphantly calling for landing-coördinates. The grid office relayed his call to loudspeaker circuits as the quickest way to get it on the communication system of the whole planet.

"*Calling ground,*" boomed the triumphant voice of the first of the student pilots Calhoun had trained. "*Calling ground! Pilot Franz in captured ship requests coördinates for landing! Purpose of landing, to deliver half a million bushels of grain captured from the enemy!*"

At first, nobody dared believe it. But the pilot could be seen on vision. He was known. No blueskin would be left alive long enough to be used as a decoy by the men of Weald! Presently the giant ship on its second voyage to Dara—the first had been a generation ago, when it threatened death and destruction—appeared as a dark pinpoint in the sky. It came down and down, and presently it hovered over the center of the tarmac, where Calhoun composedly stood on the spot where he was to have been executed.

The landing-grid crew shifted the ship to one side, and only then did Calhoun stroll in a leisurely fashion toward the Med Ship by the grid's metal-lace wall.

The big ship touched ground, and its exit-port revolved and opened, and the student pilot stood there grinning and heaving out handsful of grain. There was a swarming, yelling, deliriously triumphant crowd, then, where only minutes before there'd been a mob waiting to rejoice when Calhoun's living body exploded into flame.

They no longer hated Calhoun, but he had to fight his way to the Med Ship, nevertheless. He was surrounded by now-ecstatically admiring citizens of Dara, only minutes since they'd thirsted for his blood.

Two hours after the first ship, a second landed. Dara went wild again. Four hours later still, the third arrived. The fourth came down on the following day.

Then Calhoun faced the executive and cabinet of Dara for the second time. His tone and manner were very dry.

"Now," he said curtly, "I would like a few more astrogators to train. I think it likely that we can raid the Wealdian grain-fleet one time more, and in so doing get the beginning of a fleet for defense. I insist, however, that it must not be used in combat! We might as well be sensible about this situation! After all, four shiploads of grain won't break the famine! They'll help a lot, but they're only the beginning of what's needed for a planetary population!"

"How much grain can we hope for?" demanded a man with a blue mark covering all his chin.

Calhoun told him.

"How long before Weald can have a fleet overhead, dropping fusion bombs?" demanded another, grimly.

Calhoun named a time. But then he said;

"I think we can keep them from dropping bombs if we can get the grain-fleet and some capable astrogators."

"What do you have in mind?"

He told them. It was not possible to tell the whole story of what he considered sensible behavior. An emotional program can be presented and accepted immediately. A plan of action which is actually intelligent, considering all elements of a situation, has to be accepted piecemeal. Even so, the military men growled.

"We've plenty of heavy elements," said one, with one eye and half his forehead colored blue. "If we'd used our brains, we'd have more bombs than Weald can hope for! We could turn that whole planet into a smoking cinder!"

"Which," said Calhoun acidly, "would give you some satisfaction but not an ounce of food! And food's more important than satisfaction. Now, I'm going to take off for Weald again. I'll want somebody to build an emergency device for my ship, and I'll want the four pilots I've trained and twenty more candidates. And I'd like to have some decent rations! When the last trip brought back two million bushels of grain, you can spare adequate food for twenty men for a few days!"

It took some time to get the special device constructed, but the Med Ship lifted in two days more. The device for which it had waited was simply a preventive of the disaster overtaking the ship from the mine on Orede. It was essentially a tank of liquid oxygen, packed in the space from which stores had been taken away. When the ship's air-supply was pumped past it, first moisture and then CO_2 froze out. Then the air flowed over the liquefied oxygen at a rate to replace the CO_2 with more useful breathing material. Then the moisture was restored to the air as it warmed again. For so long as the oxygen lasted, fresh air for any number of men could be kept purified and breathable. The Med Ship's normal equipment could take care of no more than ten. But with this it could journey to Weald with almost any complement on board.

Maril stayed on Dara when the Med Ship left. Murgatroyd protested shrilly when he discovered her about to be closed out by the closing lock-door.

"*Chee!*" he said indignantly. "*Chee! Chee!*"

"No," said Calhoun, "we'll be crowded enough anyhow. We'll see her later."

He nodded to one of the first four student pilots, and he crisply made contact with the landing-grid office. He very efficiently supervised as the grid took the ship up. The other three of the four first-trained men explained every move to sub-classes assigned to each. Calhoun moved about, listening and making certain that the instruction was up to standard.

He felt queer, acting as the supervisor of an educational institution in space. He did not like it. There were twenty-four men beside himself crowded into the Med Ship's small interior. They got in each other's way. They trampled on each other. There was always somebody eating, and always somebody sleeping, and there was no need whatever for the background tape to keep the ship from being intolerably quiet. But the air-system worked well enough, except once when the reheater unit quit and the air inside the ship went down below freezing before the trouble could be found and corrected.

The journey to Weald, this time, took seven days because of the training program in effect. Calhoun bit his nails over the delay. But it was necessary for each of the students to make his own line-ups on Weald's sun, and compute distances, and for each of them to practise maneuverings that would presently be called for. Calhoun hoped desperately that preparations for active warfare—or massacre—did not move fast on Weald. He believed, however, that in the absence of direct news from Dara, Wealdian officials would take the normal course of politicos. They had proclaimed the deathship from Orede an attack from Dara. Therefore they would specialize on defensive measures before plumping for offense. They'd get patrol-ships out to spot invasion ships long before they worked on a fleet to destroy the blueskins. It would meet the public demand for defense.

Calhoun was right. The Med Ship made its final approach to Weald under Calhoun's own control. He'd made brightness-measurements on his previous journey and he used them again. They would not be strictly accurate, because a sunspot could knock all meaning out of any reading beyond two decimal places. But the first breakout was just far enough from the Wealdian system for Calhoun to be able to pick out its planets with electron telescope at maximum magnification. He could aim for Weald itself,—allowing, of course, for the lag in the apparent motion of its image because of the limited speed of light. He tried the briefest of overdrive hops, and came out within the solar system and well inside any watching patrol.

That was pure fortune. It continued. He'd broken through the screen of guard-ships in undetectable overdrive. He was within half an hour's solar-system drive of the grain-fleet. There was no alarm, at first. Of course radars spotted the Med Ship as an object, but nobody paid attention. It was not headed for Weald. It was probably assumed to be a guard-boat itself. Such mistakes do happen. It reached the grain-fleet.

Again from the storage-space from which supplies had been removed, Calhoun produced vacuum suits. The four first students went out, each escorting a less-accustomed neophyte and all fastened firmly together with space-ropes. They warmed the interiors of four ships and went on to others. Presently there were eight ships making ready for an interstellar journey, each with a scared but resolute new pilot familiarizing himself with its controls. There were sixteen ships. Twenty. Twenty-three.

A guard-ship came humming out from Weald. It would be armed, of course. It came droning, droning up the forty-odd thousand miles from the planet. Calhoun swore. He could not call his students and tell them what was happening. The guard-ship would overhear. He could not trust untried young men to act rationally if they were unwarned and the guard-ship arrived and matter-of-factly attempted to board one of them.

Then he was inspired. He called Murgatroyd, placed him before the communicator, and set it at voice-only transmission. This was familiar enough, to Murgatroyd. He'd often seen Calhoun use a communicator.

"*Chee!*" shrilled Murgatroyd. "*Chee-chee!*"

A startled voice came out of the speaker.

"*What's that?*"

"*Chee,*" said Murgatroyd zestfully.

The communicator was talking to him. Murgatroyd adored three things in order. One was Calhoun. The second was coffee. The third was pretending to converse like a human being. The speaker said explosively;

"*You there, identify yourself!*"

"*Chee-chee-chee-chee!*" observed Murgatroyd. He wriggled with pleasure and added, reasonably enough, "*Chee!*"

The communicator bawled;

"*Calling ground! Calling ground! Listen to this! Something that ain't human's talking at me on a communicator! Listen in an' tell me what to do!*"

Murgatroyd interposed with another shrill;

"*Chee!*"

Then Calhoun pulled the Med Ship slowly away from the clump of still-lifeless grain-ships. It was highly improbable that the guard-boat would carry an electron telescope. Most likely it would have only an echo-radar, and so could determine only that an object of some sort moved of its own accord in space. Calhoun let the Med Ship accelerate. That would be final evidence. The grain-ships were between Weald and its sun. Even electron telescopes on the ground— and electron-telescopes were ultimately optical telescopes with electronic amplification—even electron telescopes on the ground could not get a good image of the ship through sunlit atmosphere.

"*Chee?*" asked Murgatroyd solicitously. "*Chee-chee-chee?*"

"*Is it blueskins?*" shakily demanded the voice from the guard-boat. "*Ground! Ground! Is it blueskins?*"

A heavy, authoritative voice came in with much greater volume.

"*That's no human voice*," it said harshly. "*Approach its ship and send back an image. Don't fire first unless it heads for ground.*"

The guard-ship swerved and headed for the Med Ship. It was still a very long way off.

"*Chee-chee,*" said Murgatroyd encouragingly.

Calhoun changed the Med Ship's course. The guard-ship changed course too. Calhoun let it draw nearer,—but only a little. He led it away from the fleet of grain-ships.

He swung his electron telescope on them. He saw a space-suited figure outside one,—safely roped, however. It was easy to guess that someone had meant to return to the Med Ship for orders or to make a report, and found the Med Ship gone. He'd go back inside and turn on a communicator.

"*Chee!*" said Murgatroyd.

The heavy voice boomed;

"*You there! This is a human-occupied world! If you come in peace, cut your drive and let our guard-ship approach!*"

Murgatroyd replied in an interested but doubtful tone. The booming voice bellowed. Another voice of higher authority took over. Murgatroyd was entranced that so many people wanted to talk to him. He made what for him was practically an oration. The last voice spoke persuasively and suavely.

"*Chee-chee-chee-chee*," said Murgatroyd.

One of the grain-ships flickered and ceased to be. It had gone into overdrive. Another. And another. Suddenly they began to flick out of sight by twos and threes.

"*Chee*," said Murgatroyd with a note of finality.

The last grain-ship vanished.

"Calling guard-ship," said Calhoun drily. "This is Med ship Aesclipus Twenty. I called here a couple of weeks ago. You've been talking to my *tormal*, Murgatroyd."

A pause. A blank pause. Then profanity of deep and savage intemperance.

"I've been on Dara," said Calhoun.

Dead silence fell.

"There's a famine there," said Calhoun deliberately. "So the grain-ships you've had in orbit have been taken away by men from Dara—blueskins if you like—to feed themselves and their families. They've been dying of hunger and they don't like it."

There was a single burst of the unprintable. Then the formerly suave voice said waspishly;

"*Well? The Med Service will hear of your interference!*"

"Yes," said Calhoun. "I'll report it myself. I have a message for you. Dara is ready to pay for every ounce of grain and for the ships it was stored in. They'll pay in heavy metals,—iridium, uranium,—that sort of thing."

The suave voice fairly curdled.

"*As if we'd allow anything that was ever on Dara to touch ground here!*"

"Ah! But there can be sterilization. To begin with metals, uranium melts at 1150° centigrade, and tungsten at 3370° and iridium at 2350°. You could load such things and melt them down in space and then tow them home. And you can actually sterilize a lot of other useful materials!"

The suave voice said infuriatedly;

"I'll report this! You'll suffer for this!"

Calhoun said pleasantly;

"I'm sure that what I say is being recorded, so that I'll add that it's perfectly practical for Wealdians to land on Dara, take whatever property they think wise,—to pay for damage done by blueskins, of course—and get back to Wealdian ships with absolutely no danger of carrying contagion. If you'll make sure the recording's clear."

He described, clearly and specifically, exactly how a man could be outfitted to walk into any area of any conceivable contagion, do whatever seemed necessary in the way of looting—but Calhoun did not use the word—and then return to his fellows with no risk whatever of bringing back infection. He gave exact details. Then he said;

"My radar says you've four ships converging on me to blast me out of space. I sign off."

The Med Ship disappeared from normal space, and entered that improbably stressed area of extension which it formed about itself and in which physical constants were wildly strange. For one thing, the speed of light in overdrive-stressed space had not been measured yet. It was too high. For another, a ship could travel very many times 186000 miles per second in overdrive.

The Med Ship did just that. There was nobody but Calhoun and Murgatroyd on board. There was companionable silence,—there were only the small threshold-of-perception sounds which one did not often notice, but which it would have been intolerable to have stop.

Calhoun luxuriated in regained privacy. For seven days he'd had twenty-four other human beings crowded into the two cabins of the ship, with never so much as one yard of space between himself and someone else. One need not be snobbish to wish to be alone sometimes!

Murgatroyd licked his whiskers thoughtfully.

"I hope," said Calhoun, "that things work out right. But they may remember on Dara that I'm responsible for some ten million bushels of grain reaching them. Maybe—just possibly—they'll listen to me and act sensibly. After all, there's only one way to break a famine. Not with ten million bushels for a whole planet! And certainly not with bombs!"

Driving direct, without pausing for practisings, the Med Ship could arrive at Dara in little more than five days. Calhoun looked forward to relaxation. As a beginning he made ready to give himself an adequate meal for the first time since first landing on Dara. Then, presently, he sat down wrily to a double meal of Darian famine-rations, which were far from appetizing. But there wasn't anything else on board.

He had some pleasure later, though, envisioning what went elsewhere. On Weald, obviously, there would be purest panic. The vanishing of the grain fleet wouldn't be charged against twenty-four men. A Darian fleet would be suspected, and with the suspicion terror, and with terror a governmental crisis. Then there'd be a frantic seizure of any craft that could take to space, and the agitated improvisation of a space-fleet.

But besides that, biological-warfare technicians would examine Calhoun's instructions for equipment by which armed men could be landed on a plague-stricken planet and then safely taken off again. Military and governmental officials would come to the eminently sane conclusion that while Calhoun could not well take active measures against blueskins, as a sane and proper citizen of the galaxy he would be on the side of law and order and propriety and justice,—in short, of Weald. So they ordered sample anti-contagion suits made according to Calhoun's directions, and they had them tested. They worked admirably.

On Dara, while Calhoun journeyed back to it, grain was distributed lavishly, and everybody on the planet had their cereal ration almost doubled. It was still not a comfortable ration, but the relief was great. There was considerable gratitude felt for Calhoun, which as usual included a lively anticipation of further favors to come. Maril was interviewed repeatedly, as the person best able to discuss him, and she did his reputation no harm. That was not all that happened on Dara...

There was something else. Very curious thing, too. There was a curious spread of mild symptoms which nobody could exactly call a disease. It lasted only a few hours. A person felt slightly feverish, and ran a temperature which peaked at 30.9° centigrade, and drank more water than usual. Then his temperature went back to normal and he forgot all about it. There have always been such trivial epidemics. They are rarely recorded, because few people think to go to a doctor. That was the case here.

Calhoun looked ahead a little, too. Presently the fleet of grain-ships would arrive and unload and lift again for Orede, and this time they would make an infinity of slaughter among wild cattle-herds, and bring back incredible quantities of fresh-slaughtered frozen beef. Almost everybody would get to taste meat again, which would be most gratifying.

Then, the industries of Dara would labor at government-required tasks. An astonishing amount of fissionable material would be fashioned into bombs—a concession by Calhoun—and plastic factories make an astonishing number of plastic sag-suits. And large shipments of heavy metals in ingots would be made to the planet's capital city and there would be some guns and minor items...

Perhaps somebody could have found out any of these items in advance, but it was unlikely that anybody did. Nobody but Calhoun, however, would ever have put them together and hoped very urgently that that was the way things would work out. He could see a promising total result. In fact, in the Med ship hurtling through space, on the fourth day of his journey he thought of an improvement that could be made in the sum of all those happenings when they were put together.

He landed on Dara. Maril came to the Med Ship. Murgatroyd greeted her with enthusiasm.

"Something unusual has happened," said Maril, very much subdued. "I told you that—sometimes blueskin markings fade out on children, and then neither they nor their children ever have blueskin markings again."

"Yes," said Calhoun. "I remember."

"And you were reminded of a group of viruses on Tralee. You said they only took hold of people in terribly bad physical condition, but then they could be passed on from mother to child. Until—sometimes—they died out."

Calhoun blinked.

"Yes…"

"Korvan," said Maril very carefully, "Has worked out an idea that that's what happens to the blueskin markings on—us Darians. He thinks that people almost dead of the plague could get the—virus, and if they recovered from the plague pass the virus on and—be blueskins."

"Interesting," said Calhoun, noncommittally.

"And when we went to Weald," said Maril very carefully indeed, "you were working with some culture-material. You wrote quite a lot about it in the ship's log. You gave yourself an injection. Remember? And Murgatroyd? You wrote down your temperature, and Murgatroyd's?" She moistened her lips. "You said that if infection passed between us, something would be very infectious indeed?"

"What are you driving at?"

Maril continued slowly. "Th—thousands of people are having their pigment-spots fade away. Not only children but grownups. And—Korvan has found out that it always seems to happen after a day when they felt feverish and very thirsty—and then felt all right again. You tried out something that made you feverish and thirsty. I had it too, in the ship. Korvan thinks there's been an epidemic of something that—is obliterating the blue spots on everybody that catches it. There are always trivial epidemics that nobody notices. Korvan's found evidence of one that's making 'blueskin' no longer a word with any meaning."

"Remarkable!" said Calhoun.

"Did you—do it?" asked Maril. "Did you start a harmless epidemic that—wipes out the virus that makes blueskins?"

Calhoun said in feigned astonishment;

"How can you think such a thing, Maril?"

"Because I was there," said Maril. She said somehow desperately; "I know you did it! But the question is—are you going to tell? When people find they're not blueskins any longer—when there's no such thing as a blueskin any longer—will you tell them why?"

"Naturally not," said Calhoun. "Why?" Then he guessed. "Has Korvan—"

"He thinks," said Maril, "that he thought it up all by himself. He's found the proof. He's—very proud. I'd have to tell him the truth if you were going to tell. And he'd be ashamed and—angry."

Calhoun considered, staring at her.

"How it happened doesn't matter," he said at last. "The idea of anybody doing it deliberately would be disturbing, too. It shouldn't get about. So it seems much the best thing for

Korvan to discover what's happened to the blueskin pigment, and how it happened, but not why."

She read his face carefully.

"You aren't doing it as a favor to me," she decided. "You'd rather it was that way."

She looked at him for a long time, until he squirmed. Then she nodded and went away.

An hour later the Wealdian space-fleet was reported, massed in space and driving for Dara.

CHAPTER EIGHT

There were small scout-ships which came on ahead of the main fleet. They'd originally been guard-boats, intended for solar-system duty only and quite incapable of overdrive. They'd come from Weald in the cargo-holds of the liners now transformed into fighting ships. The scouts swept low, transmitting fine-screen images back to the fleet, of all that they might see before they were shot down. They found the landing-grid. It contained nothing larger than Calhoun's Med Ship, Aesclipus Twenty.

They searched here and there. They flitted to and fro, scanning wide bands of the surface of Dara. The planet's cities and highways and industrial centers were wholly open to inspection from the sky. It looked as if the scouts hunted most busily for the fleet of former grain-ships which Calhoun had said blueskins had seized and rushed away. If the scouts looked for them, they did not find them.

Dara offered no opposition to the scout-ships. Nothing rose to space to oppose or to resist their search. They went darting over every portion of the hungry planet, land and seas alike, and there was no sign of military preparedness against their coming. The huge ships of the main fleet waited while they reported monotonously that they saw no sign of the stolen fleet. But the stolen fleet was the only means by which the planet could be defended. There could be no point in a pitched battle in emptiness. But a fleet with a planet to back it might be dangerous.

Hours passed. The Wealdian main fleet waited. There was no offensive movement by the fleet. There was no defensive action from the ground, With fusion-bombs certain to be involved in any actual conflict, there was something like an embarrassed pause. The Wealdian ships were ready to bomb. They were less anxious to be vaporized by possible suicide-dashes of defending ships who might blow themselves up near contact with their enemies.

But a fleet cannot travel some light-years through space to make a mere threat. And the Wealdian fleet was furnished with the material for total devastation. It could drop bombs from hundreds, or thousands, or even tens of thousands of miles away. It could cover the world of Dara with mushroom clouds springing up and spreading to make a continuous pall of atomic-fusion products. And they could settle down and kill every living thing not destroyed by the explosions themselves. Even the creatures of the deepest oceans would die of deadly, purposely-contrived fallout particles.

The Wealdian fleet contemplated its own destructiveness. It found no capacity for defense on Dara. It moved forward.

But then a message went out from the capital city of Dara. It said that a ship in overdrive had carried word to a Darian fleet in space. The Darian fleet now hurtled toward Weald. It was a fleet of thirty-seven giant ships. They carried such-and-such bombs in such-and-such quantities. Unless its orders were countermanded, it would deliver those bombs on Weald—set to explode. If Weald bombed Dara, the orders could not be withdrawn. So Weald could bomb Dara. It could destroy all life on the pariah planet. But Weald would die with it.

The fleet ceased its advance. The situation was a stalemate with pure desperation on one side and pure frustration on the other. This was no way to end the war. Neither planet could trust the other, even for minutes. If they did not destroy each other simultaneously, as now was possible, each would expect the other to launch an unwarned attack at some other moment. Ultimately one or the other must perish, and the survivor would be the one most skilled in treachery.

But then the pariah planet made a new proposal. It would send a messenger-ship to stop its own fleet's bombardment if Weald would accept payment for the grain-ships and their cargoes. It would pay in ingots of iridium and uranium and tungsten—and gold if Weald wished it—for all damages Weald might claim. It would even pay indemnity for the miners of Orede, who had died by accident but perhaps in some sense through its fault. It would pay... But if it were bombed, Weald must spout atomic fire and the fleet of Weald would have no home planet to return to.

This proposal seemed both craven and foolish. It would allow the fleet of Weald to loot and then betray Dara. But it was Calhoun's idea. It seemed plausible to the admirals of Weald. They felt only contempt for blueskins. Contemptuously, they accepted the semi-surrender.

The broadcast waves of Dara told of agreement, and wild and fierce resentment filled the pariah planet's people. There was almost—almost!—revolution to insist upon resistance, however hopeless and however fatal. But not all of Dara realized that a vital change had come about in the state of things on Dara. The enemy fleet had not a hint of it. And therefore—

In menacing array, the invading fleet spread itself about the skies of Dara, well beyond the atmosphere. Harsh voices talked with increasing arrogance to the landing-grid staff. A monster ship of Weald came heavily down, riding the landing-grid's force-fields. It touched gently. Its occupants were apprehensive, but hungry for the loot they had been assured was theirs. The ship's outer hull would be sterilized before it returned to Weald, of course. And there was adequate protection for the landing-party.

Men came out of the ship's ports. They wore the double, transparent sag-suits Calhoun had suggested, which had been painstakingly tested, and which were perfect protection against contagion. They could loot with impunity, and all contamination would remain outside the suits. What loot they gathered, obviously, could be decontaminated before it was returned to Weald. It was a most satisfactory discovery, to realize that blueskins could be not only scorned but robbed. There was only one bit of relevant information the space-fleet of Weald did not have.

That information was that the people of Dara weren't blueskins any longer. There'd been a trivial epidemic.

The sag-suited men of Weald went zestfully about their business. They took over the landing-grid's operation, driving the Darian operators away. For the first time in history the operators of a landing-grid wore makeup to look like they did have blue pigment in their skins. The Wealdian landing-party tested the grid's operation. They brought down another giant ship. Then another. And another.

Parties in the shiny sag-suits spread through the city. There were the huge stock-piles of precious metals, brought in readiness to be surrendered and carried away. Some men set to work to load these into the holds—to be sterilized later. Some went forthrightly after personal loot.

They came upon very few Darians. Those they saw kept sullenly away from them. They entered shops and took what they fancied. They zestfully removed the treasure of banks.

Triumphal and scornful reports went up to the hovering great ships. The blueskins, said the reports were spiritless and cowardly. They permitted themselves to be robbed. They kept out of the way. It had been observed that the population was streaming out of the city, fleeing because they feared the ships' landing-parties. The blueskins had abjectly produced all they'd promised of precious metals, but there was more to be taken.

More ships came down, and more. Some of the first, heavily loaded, were lifted to emptiness again and the process of decontamination of their hulls began. There was jealousy among the ships in space for those upon the ground. The first-landed ships had had their choice of loot. There were squabblings about priorities, now that the navy of Weald plainly had a license to steal. There was confusion among the members of the landing-parties. Discipline disappeared. Men in plastic sag-suits roved about as individuals, seeking what they might loot.

There were armed and alerted landing-parties around the grid itself, of course, but the capital city of Dara lay open. Men coming back with loot found their ships already lifted off to make room for others. They were pushed into reëmbarking-parties of other ships. There were more and more men to be found on ships where they did not belong, and more and more not to be found where they did. By the time half the fleet had been aground, there was no longer any pretense of holding a ship down until all its crew returned. There were too many other ships' companies clamoring for their turn to loot. The rosters of many ships, indeed, bore no particular relationship to the men actually on board.

There were less than fifteen ships whose to-be-fumigated holds were still empty, when the watchful government of Dara broadcast a new message to the invaders. It requested that the looting stop. No matter what payment Weald claimed, it had taken payment five times over. Now was time to stop.

It was amusing. The space-admiral of Weald ordered his ships alerted for action. The message-ship, ordering the Darian fleet away from Weald, had been sent off long since. No other ship could get away now! The Darians could take their choice; accept the consequences of surrender, or the fleet would rise to throw down bombs.

Calhoun was asking politely to be taken to the Wealdian admiral when the trouble began. It wasn't on the ground, at all. Everything was under splendid control where a landing-force occupied the grid and all the ground immediately about it. The space admiral had headquarters in the landing-grid office. Reports came in, orders were issued, admirably crisp salutes were exchanged among sag-suited men… Everything was in perfect shape there.

But there was panic among the ships in space. Communicators gave off horrified, panic-stricken yells. There were screamings. Intelligible communications ceased. Ships plunged crazily this way and that. Some vanished in overdrive. At least one plunged at full power into a Darian ocean.

The space-admiral found himself in command of fifteen ships only, out of all his former force. The rest of the fleet went through a period of hysterical madness. In some ships it lasted for minutes only. In others it went on for half an hour or more. Then they hung overhead, but did not reply to calls.

Calhoun arrived at the space-port with Murgatroyd riding on his shoulder. A bewildered officer in a sag-suit halted him.

"I've come," said Calhoun, "to speak to the admiral. My name is Calhoun and I'm Med Service, and I think I met the Admiral at a banquet a few weeks ago. He'll remember me."

"You'll have to wait," protested the officer. "There's some trouble—"

"Yes," said Calhoun. "I know about it. I helped design it. I want to explain it to the admiral. He needs to know what's happened, if he's to take appropriate measures."

There were jitterings. Many men in sag-suits had still no idea that anything had gone wrong. Some appeared, brightly carrying loot. Some hung eagerly around the airlocks of ships on the grid tarmac, waiting their turns to stand in corrosive gases for the decontamination of their suits, when they would burn the outer layers and step, aseptic and happy, into a Wealdian ship again. There they could think how rich they were going to be back on Weald.

But the situation aloft was bewildering and very, very ominous. There was strident argument. Presently Calhoun stood before the Wealdian admiral.

"I came to explain something," said Calhoun pleasantly. "The situation has changed. You've noticed it, I'm sure."

The admiral glared at him through two layers of plastic, which covered him almost like a gift-wrapped parcel.

"Be quick!" he rasped.

"First," said Calhoun, "there are no more blueskins. An epidemic of something or other has made the blue patches on the skins of Darians fade out. There have always been some who didn't have blue patches. Now nobody has them."

"Nonsense!" rasped the admiral. "And what has that got to do with this situation?"

"Why, everything," said Calhoun mildly. "It means that Darians can pass for Wealdians whenever they please. That they are passing for Wealdians. That they've been mixing with your men, wearing sag-suits exactly like the one you're wearing now. They've been going aboard your ships in the confusion of returning looters. There's not a ship now aloft, that has been aground today, that hasn't from one to fifteen Darians—no longer blueskins—on board."

The admiral roared. Then his face turned gray.

"You can't take your fleet back to Weald," said Calhoun gently, "if you believe its crews have been exposed to carriers of the Dara plague. You wouldn't be allowed to land, anyhow."

The admiral said through stiff lips;

"I'll blast—"

"No," said Calhoun, again gently. "When you ordered all ships alerted for action, the Darians on each ship released panic-gas. They only needed tiny, pocket-sized containers of the gas for the job. They had them. They only needed to use air-tanks from their sag-suits to protect themselves against the gas. They kept them handy. On nearly all your ships aloft your crews are crazy from panic-gas. They'll stay that way until the air is changed. Darians have barricaded themselves in the control-rooms of most if not all your ships. You haven't got a fleet. If the few ships that will obey your orders, drop one bomb, our fleet off Weald will drop fifty. I don't think you'd better order offensive action. Instead, I think you'd better have your fleet medical officers come and learn some of the facts of life. There's no need for war between Dara and Weald, but if you insist…"

The Admiral made a choking noise. He could have ordered Calhoun killed, but there was a certain appalling fact. The men aground from the fleet were breathing Wealdian air from tanks. It would last so long only. If they were taken on board the still obedient ships overhead, Darians would unquestionably be mixed with them. There was no way to take off the parties now aground without exposing them to contact with Darians, on the ground or in the ships. There was no way to sort out the Darians.

"I—I will give the orders," said the admiral thickly. "I— do not know what you devils plan, but—I don't know how to stop you."

"All that's necessary," said Calhoun warmly, "is an open mind. There's a misunderstanding to be cleared up, and some principles of planetary health practises to be explained, and a certain amount of prejudice that has to be thrown away. But nobody need die of changing their minds. The Interstellar Medical service has proved that over and over!"

Murgatroyd, perched on his shoulder, felt that it was time to take part in the conversation. He said;

"*Chee-chee!*"

"Yes," agreed Calhoun. "We do want to get the job done. We're behind schedule now."

It was not, of course, possible for Calhoun to leave immediately. He had to preside at various meetings of the medical officers of the fleet with the health officials of Dara. He had to make explanations, and correct misapprehensions, and delicately suggest such biological experiments as would prove to the doctors of Weald that there was no longer a plague on Dara, whatever had been the case three generations before. He had to sit by while an extremely self-confident young Darian doctor named Korvan rather condescendingly demonstrated that the former blue pigmentation was a viral product quite unconnected with the plague, and that it had been wiped out by a very trivial epidemic of—such and such. Calhoun regarded that young man with a detached interest. Maril thought him wonderful, even if she had to give him the material for his work. Calhoun shrugged and went on with his work:

The return of loot. Mutual, full, and complete agreement that Darians were no longer carriers of plague, if they had ever been. Unless Weald convinced other worlds of this, Weald itself would join Dara in isolation from neighboring worlds. A messenger ship to recall the twenty-seven ships once floating in orbit about Weald. Most of them would be used for some time, now, to bring beef from Orede. Some would haul more grain from Weald. It would be paid for. There would be a need for commercial missions to be exchanged between Weald and Dara.

It was a full week before he could go to the little Med Ship and prepare for departure. Even then there were matters to be attended to. All the food-supplies that had been removed could not be replaced. There were biological samples to be replaced and some to be destroyed... The air-tanks...

Maril came to the Med Ship again when he was almost ready to leave. She did not seem comfortable.

"I wish you could like Korvan," she said regretfully.

"I don't dislike him," said Calhoun. "I think he will be a most prominent citizen, in time. He has all the talents for it."

Maril smiled very faintly.

"But you don't admire him."

"I wouldn't say that," protested Calhoun. "After all, he is attractive to you, which is something I couldn't manage."

"You didn't try," said Maril. "Just as I didn't try to be fascinating to you. Why?"

Calhoun spread out his hands. But he looked at Maril with respect. Not every woman could have faced the fact that a man did not feel impelled to make passes at her. It is simply a fact that has nothing to do with desirability or charm or anything else.

"You're going to marry him," he said. "I hope you'll be very happy."

"He's the man I want," said Maril frankly. "He looks forward to splendid discoveries. I'm sorry it's so important to him."

Calhoun did not ask the obvious question. Instead, he said thoughtfully;

"There's something you could do... It needs to be done. The Med Service in this sector has been badly handled. There are a number of—discoveries that need to be made. I don't think your Korvan would relish having things handed to him on a visible silver platter. But they should be known…"

Maril said wrily;

"I can guess what you mean. I never went into detail about how the blueskin markings disappeared, but a few hints—You've got books for me?"

Calhoun nodded. He brought them to her.

"If we only fell in love with each other, Maril, we'd be a team! Too bad! These are a wedding present you'll do well to hide."

She put her hands in his.

"I like you—almost as much as I like Murgatroyd! Yes! Korvan will never know, and he'll be a great man." Then she added defensively, "And not just from these books! He'll make his own wonderful discoveries."

"Of which," said Calhoun, "the most remarkable is you. Good luck Maril!"

Presently the Med Ship lifted. Calhoun aimed it for the next planet on the list of those he was to visit. After this one more he'd return to sector headquarters with a biting report to make on the way things had been handled before him. He said;

"Overdrive coming, Murgatroyd!"

Then the stars went out and there was silence, and privacy, and a faint, faint, almost unhearable series of background sounds which kept the Med Ship from being totally unendurable.

Long, long days later the ship broke out of overdrive and Calhoun guided it to a round and sunlit world. In due time he thumped the communicator-button.

"Calling ground," he said crisply. "Calling ground! Med Ship Aesclipus Twenty reporting arrival and asking coördinates for landing. Purpose of landing, planetary health inspection. Our mass is fifty standard tons."

There was a pause while the beamed message went many, many thousands of miles. Then the speaker said;

"*Aesclipus Twenty, repeat your identification!*"

Murgatroyd said;

"*Chee-chee? Chee?*"

Calhoun sighed.

"That's right, Murgatoryd! Here we go again!!

THE END

If you've enjoyed this book, you will not want to miss these terrific titles...

ARMCHAIR SCI-FI, FANTASY, & HORROR DOUBLE NOVELS, $12.95 each

D-41   **FULL CYCLE** by Clifford D. Simak
       IT WAS THE DAY OF THE ROBOT by Frank Belknap Long

D-42   **REIGN OF THE TELEPUPPETS** by Daniel Galouye
       THIS CROWDED EARTH by Robert Bloch

D-43   **THE CRISPIN AFFAIR** by Jack Sharkey
       THE RED HELL OF JUPITER by Paul Ernst

D-44   **PLANET OF DREAD** by Dwight V. Swain
       WE THE MACHINE by Gerald Vance

D-45   **THE STAR HUNTER** by Edmond Hamilton
       THE ALIEN by Raymond F. Jones

D-46   **WORLD OF IF** by Rog Phillips
       SLAVE RAIDERS FROM MERCURY by Don Wilcox

D-47   **THE ULTIMATE PERIL** by Robert Abernathy
       PLANET OF SHAME by Bruce Elliot

D-48   **THE FLYING EYES** by J. Hunter Holly
       SOME FABULOUS YONDER by Phillip Jose Farmer

D-49   **THE COSMIC BUNGLARS** by Geoff St. Reynard
       THE BUTTONED SKY by Geoff St. Reynard

D-50   **TYRANTS OF TIME** by Milton Lesser
       PARIAH PLANET by Murray Leinster

ARMCHAIR SCIENCE FICTION CLASSICS, $12.95 each

C-13   **SUNKEN WORLD**
       by Stanton A. Coblentz

C-14   **THE LAST VIAL**
       by Sam McClatchie, M. D.

C-15   **WE WHO SURVIVED (THE FIFTH ICE AGE)**
       by Sterling Noel

ARMCHAIR MASTERS OF SCIENCE FICTION SERIES, $16.95 each

MS-5   **MASTERS OF SCIENCE FICTION, Vol. Five**
       Winston K. Marks—Test Colony and other tales

MS-6   **MASTERS OF SCIENCE FICTION, Vol. Six**
       Fritz Leiber—Deadly Moon and other tales